SILENT SOULS

GWYN BENNETT

Storm

ALSO BY GWYN BENNETT

Dr Harrison Lane Mysteries

1. *Broken Angels*

2. *Beautiful Remains*

3. *Deadly Secrets*

4. *Innocent Dead*

5. *Perfect Beauties*

6. *Captive Heart*

7. *Winter Graves*

8. *Dark Whispers*

9. *Burning Lies*

Saskia Monet Series

1. *The Stolen Ones*

2. *Secrets in the Blood*

3. *Island of Graves*

DI Clare Falle Series

1. *Lonely Hearts*

2. *Home Help*

3. *Death Bond*

The Villagers

Dead End

ONE

'What the hell are we doing!' Ellie Robertson's voice, slightly breathless from the hill climb, was strained with exasperation.

'Thirtieth anniversary. Here for the celebratory party, aren't we? Not quite as fit as we used to be though, ay?' Phil Stevenson had always been the one to come back with the cynical quips.

Ellie was more than aware that she wasn't as thin as she used to be without him pointing it out.

'We're all here because our great leader has requested our presence,' Dermot's relaxed Irish lilt came from the rear of the group.

'Less requested, more blackmailed,' Ellie muttered.

'Former great leader, and he's not even here! Where is he? I suppose you still believe all that stuff?' Phil ignored Ellie's comment and turned round to look at Dermot, who had embellished his jeans and jacket by wrapping a striped sarong around his waist. His long hair, earrings, and the leather strung pendant he wore, further evidence of his slightly alternative lifestyle.

'You're right, this is ridiculous. I haven't seen any of you in decades,' Dermot hit back, ignoring the barbed personal comment, 'and yet here we all are!'

'I swore I'd never come back here, not after the last time,' Ellie whined at the other five, who had all stopped momentarily. 'What did he mean about new evidence of what really happened back then? We know the truth.'

'So why are you here then?' Dermot asked her, raising one of his thick black eyebrows. 'Why are any of us here?'

There was no answer from any of them, but they didn't turn back. Instead the group fell silent for the remaining five minutes' climb until they came to the bushes that they knew hid the entrance to the cave.

'Jordan must be here already, he's cut back some of the brambles,' Andy said to the group. He scanned the ground before bending and picking up a large stick. 'I'll hold the rest back.' He pushed the thorny brambles away, revealing a dark entrance. One by one, the group turned on their phone lights, or took torches from their pockets, and squeezed through the gap Andy had created between the stones and bushes.

'Bloody hell the smell of this place brings it all back,' Paige Nicholson had followed Phil and Ellie into the dark interior, immediately coming to a halt in a small rocky entrance way, where the natural daylight just about managed to reach. She sniffed at the damp, slightly mouldy air.

'Been here thousands of years, not likely to alter much over the last thirty,' Dermot said as he too entered into the darkness. 'We are but a millisecond in the history of the world. Inconsequential in the great scheme of nature. Fleas on the back of the elephant.'

'Thought you said earlier that we were destroying it with our petrol cars and consumerism,' Phil hit back.

'Yeah, we are. But that's all we're good for. Destruction.'

'Well not quite so inconsequential then, are we?'

'So where's Jordan then?' Kelly interrupted the philosophical debate before it could turn into an argument, her voice clipped and impatient.

'I can take a pretty good guess, can't you?' Phil replied, holding his phone torch high to scan the small chamber that they now all stood in. He then fixed the beam on the rock corridor leading away from it and set off.

As he walked, he called out, 'Jordan. Jordan, you in here?'

'What do you think it's going to be?' Paige whispered to Dermot as they followed. 'This evidence that he's discovered and which we all need to see...'

'Who knows, but it beats sitting at home on the sofa watching some shite on the box.'

The corridor was narrow, and at times they had to squeeze around rocks or duck as the ceiling lowered.

'Don't remember it being this much of a squeeze back then,' Ellie mumbled.

Dermot hmphed but didn't state the obvious: that most of them, and particularly Ellie, had expanded somewhat since their late teens.

The last remnants of daylight were behind them, leaving their torches to pick out the limestone-stained rocks and ghostly white shadows of stalactites hanging like mid-air fangs from above. Occasionally a drip of water would catch one of their eyes, movement in the dark that made a heart skip, until the plop of its landing amidst all the drops that had fallen before it, calmed the nerves. As they walked, the air grew colder. Damp and hanging heavy, wrapping their skin with its cool caress.

'What's that?' Kelly stopped suddenly, turning and peering past Ellie, Dermot and Andy in the rear. The four of them listened. 'I heard footsteps behind us.'

'Me too. Maybe Jordan isn't here yet,' Andy offered. 'Jordan!' He called out, peering into the darkness, looking for Jordan's blond head to appear in the light of his torch beam.

Nothing.

'Let's catch up with the others,' Kelly's voice was unusually slightly breathless, betraying her nerves. She started walking again, faster this time as she tried to catch up with Paige's fast-disappearing back.

As the darkness threatened to become all encompassing, flickering candlelight at the end of the corridor of rock appeared up ahead, followed by surprised exclamations from those at the head of the group.

They'd all entered a large, domed chamber of rock. Around the edges, stalactites grew down from the ceiling as though the roots of some albino carrots planted above had found their way into this underground chamber. The drip-drip sound of water from their tips magnified as it bounced off the bare rock faces, confusing the ears and the mind. In places, stalagmites grew up to meet their cousins from above, sharing their mineral-rich water. Hundreds, or in most case, thousands of years' worth of steady growth.

But it wasn't the natural wonders which caught their attention. In the centre of the chamber was a wooden statue of an Egyptian god, around which big candles in earthenware jars were placed. The statue had the body of a man, with the head of an animal with big ears and a long nose. It wore a loin cloth and held some kind of sceptre or spear and a hoop-topped cross. In front of the statue was a large wooden board that carried an inverse pentagram, surrounded by a circle, and painted in silver.

'It's just like back then,' Ellie whispered, expressing all their thoughts. She shivered, unsure if it was the lower temperature of the caves or the thread of fear which coursed through her. 'I thought the police had all this removed.'

'They did!' Andy replied as the six of them stared at the scene.

The candlelight danced around the walls of the cave, showing Egyptian hieroglyphics and crude paintings on the surface of the rock. A primitive altar sat at the feet of the statue.

'What's he playing at?' Phil said scornfully. 'Does he seriously think he can persuade us to start this up all over again? We're not bloody kids anymore.'

Just then, Paige gasped and pointed towards the way they had just come. A white mist was curling its way from the mouth of the entrance, and into the chamber in which they stood, as though it had followed in their wake.

'What's that? Where's that come from?'

'Right, I've had enough,' Phil said. 'He's not even here. I'm —' But he didn't finish his sentence.

A deep growl came from the mist, rumbling around the cave system.

Ellie whimpered and all six moved closer together.

'That was behind us,' Andy said, moving away from the corridor exit.

'I'm scared.' Paige clasped her arms around her torso tightly.

'It's probably just thunder. The weather must have changed outside and that's why the mist has dropped.' Phil's face looked confident enough, but the tightness in his jaw and his voice betrayed him.

'Didn't sound like thunder, sounded like a growl. Maybe he's angry,' Ellie whispered, nodding towards the statue.

'Really? You believe that? Your imagination's working over-time because of where we are,' Phil countered.

Nobody else said anything as they looked from one to another as they tried to work out what to do next.

Declan wandered up to the cave walls, peering at the hiero-glyphs. 'This looks like blood! I think these have been painted in blood,' he said, his voice raising an octave as he turned round to the others; but nobody replied because it was at this point that they heard something else.

'Help, I need your help!' A voice seemed to come from nowhere. 'Phil, Andy, you there?'

'That's Jordan,' Paige said, looking all around them, as

though Jordan could be in the rock chamber with them and simply not be seen.

All six of them scanned each other's faces, looking to see if they knew what was going on, and critically if they were going to run or try and find him.

Another rumbling growl echoed from the entrance corridor.

'What do we do?' Ellie asked.

'Well I'm about to shit myself,' Dermot offered.

'You always were a coward,' Phil snapped at him. 'You were the first out last time.'

'Yeah? Well you weren't far behind, mate,' Dermot hit back. 'I could feel your breath on my neck.'

'This is probably a big joke; Jordan's set all this up,' Andy offered, trying to prevent the group from going into panic mode.

'You're right. He's trying to put the wind up us. It's one big joke. He got us here. I've had enough.'

'Help me, please, don't leave me!' Jordan's voice echoed around the chamber, just as Phil turned towards the exit.

'What if he's really in trouble?' Paige said to them. 'We can't leave him. Not like before.'

Phil hesitated. 'He's got to be in the small chamber at the back,' he said, shining his phone torch through the only other gap in the rock face. 'Come on then.' He stepped forward and turned to look back at the rest of the group who were still standing watching him. 'Well we doing this? Or you gonna just walk out and leave him? I bet we're going to get in there and he's going to be standing there laughing at us, having recorded the whole thing on video, at which point I'll probably deck him.'

'I don't get where that's coming from and what's making that noise?' Kelly said nodding towards the swirling mist which was now pouring into the chamber. She looked at the statue as though it would give her the answer.

'I'm not going to leave Jordan,' Andy said ignoring her and

stepping forward. The rest of them all knew exactly why he wouldn't, their minds going back thirty years.

Watching the two alpha males of the group move to leave the chamber and not wanting to be the first to walk back through the swirling mist, prompted the others to huddle after them.

'What if we get stuck in here?' Ellie whimpered.

'We've got mobile phones this time,' Paige replied, waggling her phone.

'We won't get a signal in here, not with all this rock around us,' Kelly said to her, exasperated, and prompting them to look at their handsets. She was right.

Up ahead, a string of expletives from Phil re-centred their attention and within seconds all of them were in the smaller chamber staring at what appeared to be a man, tied to the rock face at the back. Only they couldn't see his face because on his head was a mask. The same head that stood atop the statue in the main chamber. The mask of Egyptian god, Set.

Like the statue, it was mostly black, with a long nose that sloped downwards and long square topped ears. The eyes were lined by gold and what appeared to be a headdress or hair which flowed down the back of the head.

It took a few moments for them to register what they were looking at. The man, wearing jeans and a pale blue jumper, was tied, star-like to the wall. As they walked in, he lifted his masked head. Behind the mask they saw wild, staring eyes and white clammy skin.

'Jordan?' Phil stepped towards him. 'What the hell?'

Jordan attempted to wriggle in his bondage, but he was tied too tightly, and so made noises like swallowed screams.

'We've got you, mate, hang on,' Phil replied.

Andy and Phil both stepped forward together towards the stricken man who, with each step, seemed to strain against his ropes even more frantically.

The rest of the group edged forward with them, but they were just three feet away from reaching the man when the ground suddenly exploded.

Sand flew up in a big cloud, almost obliterating their view of the man, flying into their eyes, instantly making them water and sticking to their lashes; and making them turn their heads away.

A whoosh sound was followed by a sickening crunch as metal crushed flesh and bone.

As if from nowhere, a huge spike had shot out of the ground and slammed into Jordan's chest.

As the dust settled, all six blinked disbelievingly through gritted eyes at what was in front of them.

Time was suspended as brains caught up with what their eyes were telling them.

For a few seconds, there was silence apart from the gurgling last breaths of Jordan Oaks.

Then Paige and Ellie screamed.

Ellie started babbling hysterically. 'I told you, he's here. He's angry... He's going to kill us all.'

Chaos erupted.

Every one of them ran. Bumping into each other in their blind panic and haste to get out through the main chamber, the white mist filling it as though it was coming from the walls, climbing up and curling down from the roof.

As they scrambled back along the corridor towards the exit, breath coming fast and loud, behind them they heard another deep growl.

More screams as they jostled to escape.

Scraping hands, banging heads, tripping.

Ellie fell, slipping on loose shingle face-first into the ground, banging her chin on a rock. Andy, just behind, managed to avoid trampling on her and hauled her up, not stopping to check her, but half dragging her out of the cave as he went.

It seemed like an eternity in that dark tunnel, before

they burst out into the pale sunlight, not caring about the brambles this time, scratching their faces and hands, ripping their clothing, and tumbling back down the hill path to their cars.

The second they were free from the cave, Phil and Kelly were on their mobile phones calling the police. Squinting at their handsets as they tried to see through gritty eyes.

Andy was still helping Ellie, who seemed to have lost all ability to think independently.

They all continued to slip and trip down the rough path, constantly turning back to ensure that nobody or nothing was following them.

Kelly, still on the phone, wasn't concentrating on her footing, and slipped. She tried to save herself, but instead went flying, spilling several feet down the hillside where she ended up sprawled on her front.

'Quick,' Dermot said as he helped her up, his relaxed Irish drawl replaced with a harsh command.

'My phone,' Kelly said, peering through streaming eyes for evidence of where her mobile had been flung.

'I'm not staying to look for that,' Dermot said to her and headed back down the hill with the others.

Kelly spent a few more seconds trying to see where the phone had landed, but the fast-disappearing voices of her companions coupled with her limited vision, and the memory of what they had just experienced, was too much and she made the quick decision to leave her phone.

'Ow, ow!' Each step down the hill created searing pain in her ankle. She was angry as well as terrified by the time her red BMW came into view, and she wasn't the only one.

'What the hell just happened?' Ellie was squealing at the top of her voice. 'I mean, what the hell! Is he dead? Was that for real?' She was rubbing at her eyes, along with the rest of them, trying to get the sand and dust out. 'I told you, it's Set,' Ellie said again, hysterically. She was shaking, shock already taking over her body.

'It looked real and I don't think you get a bloody great big metal spike through your chest and survive, do you?' Dermot replied. He had a bottle of water and was tipping it into his eyes, head back.

Nobody challenged her about Set.

'I'm outta here,' Dermot said to them, shaking the water off and heading towards his electric moped.

'I knew I shouldn't have come,' Kelly said aloud. 'I don't know if I can even drive back.'

'I can't believe he's dead... I mean I just can't believe it,' Paige mumbled, pacing around the small car park. 'Who, what...'

Dermot started up his scooter.

'What are you doing? You can't leave,' Phil, who had been finishing his phone call, shouted at him. 'The police are on their way.'

'I'm not staying here, not with—' Dermot looked to the hill.

'He might come for us,' Ellie squeaked, fumbling in her pocket for her car keys.

'Shut up and calm down. All of you,' Phil commanded them. 'The police are going to be here in about ten minutes. This can't be like last time. I've got a career, a family, a reputation. This time we need to get our stories straight or they're not going to believe us. They're not stupid, they'll know about what happened before.' He scanned the pale faces in front of him. 'Do you understand! I don't know what just happened in there, but it's got nothing to do with me and my life. I'm not going to get dragged through the mud for this. This time we have to get it right.' He looked towards Kelly. She'd been the one who'd taken charge last time. They might need her to again.

TWO

Harrison Lane stood studying the police detective in front of him, who was clearly feeling totally out of his comfort zone.

'They're being very uncooperative,' Detective Sergeant Gavin Potter was saying, waving his arm around presumably to indicate the people who lived in the small rural village. 'I mean it's not my fault their local station was closed. Cost cutting. That's way above my pay grade, but it's like we're bloody aliens the way they're treating us. Complete ignorance, that's what it is. They just don't live in the real world.'

The officer was in his late thirties and Harrison would hazard a guess that this was one of his first investigations where he was in charge. A seemingly low-risk crime that involved criminal damage was, however, fast turning into a major headache and a national news story for what appeared to be its paranormal goings on, with talk of a dark devil spirit roaming the graveyard and village. The interest from the media was what had prompted the Detective Superintendent, boss of the detective in front of him, to call in the help of Dr Harrison Lane, head of the Ritualistic Behavioural Crime unit. It was starting to become an embarrassment for them.

'What about the homeowner?' Harrison asked. 'Didn't she contact you too?'

'Yes, she's alright. Only moved here from London about a month or so ago. Talking about moving back again now. She probably thinks they've moved into some kind of horror movie. Don't blame her.'

'But it was her boys who did the Ouija board?'

DS Potter nodded. 'Ever since then the beast has been terrorising them and attacking the church and graveyard. I can't see a rational explanation. We've had patrol cars on the street here the last two nights but seen nothing, no one, and yet in the morning there's more damage.'

'And you've discounted the boys?'

'They both went back to boarding school last week. It's still happening.'

Harrison nodded thoughtfully.

'I don't mind telling you it's giving me the creeps. Those claw marks on the door...' The detective dropped his voice to a whisper. 'They're not natural. I thought this was going to be bored kids during their half-term break, but I can't explain it, something else is going on here and it's not human.'

'I'll take a look,' Harrison said, not rising to the man's superstitious fears.

'I'll show you,' the detective replied, moving off with him.

'No. I'll go alone. Helps the concentration,' Harrison politely but firmly insisted.

The detective gave a brief nod, no doubt relieved that he didn't have to go back into the churchyard.

There was a small wooden arch and gate into the church grounds, all of which had seen better days. A small notice inside the entrance told Harrison that the church was only used occasionally for festivals and the like, and that villagers had to travel to one of two other nearby churches for their regular worship. It didn't surprise him. Thousands of little English churches had closed over the last decade as congregations shrank and their upkeep became too much for the church and local community to carry. Now, less than half of the population called themselves Christian, and atheism had become the norm. It didn't stop people from being superstitious though, that much was clear from his busy workload; but that had been human nature for as long as people had existed, no matter which religion was in vogue at the time.

Harrison walked through and into the churchyard where he stopped and stood for a few moments. Not moving, just looking. Breathing. Taking it all in.

He saw the church, grey stone with a dark grey slate roof. An arched wooden door at the front, and a little bell tower to call the villagers to worship. It was a classic rural village church, small and simple in its design and build, no big expensive stained-glass windows. All an indication that it had been likely funded by someone locally for the farm workers around the area.

There were no grand mausoleums in the churchyard, no big stone monuments to those who had gone before. The gravestones were old, bleached and covered in algae. The history of the village was here to read. In the names of the children, lost to illnesses now eradicated from British society; in the men who gave their lives for their country in one of the Great Wars; and in the family surnames which were repeated generation after generation. Harrison wondered how many of their modern-day descendants still lived locally.

Before he moved on, Harrison turned and looked further out from the churchyard, at the surrounding area. To his right was a pretty stone house, probably the former vicarage, where the woman from London and her teenage boys lived. To the left, a small field sloped downwards, and if he wasn't mistaken, a stream ran along at the bottom. Beyond, there were the roofs of the rest of the village, undulating grey waves below the autumn sky.

Once he had the lay of the land, Harrison turned his attention to the details. First, he walked around the graveyard. It wasn't in advanced disrepair, not like the cemetery in his childhood nightmares, Nunhead in London, where he'd witnessed a friend's ritualistic murder. But neither was it neat and well used, although someone clearly tried to keep it relatively tidy so that it didn't become completely overgrown; and it hadn't fallen victim to vandalism – until now.

As Harrison walked towards the right, he saw the fallen gravestones and sunken grave markers that were causing the upset. A stone cross lay prone on top of another headstone that had cracked from its impact. The ground was sunken in, as though something had crawled from a grave and left an empty cavity in its absence. He could see the corner of a coffin, disturbed and broken.

At the site of the damage Harrison crouched down, scanning the earth for signs using the tracking techniques taught to him by his native American stepfather, one of the Shadow Wolves who patrolled the US borders. He looked closely at the ground and the patterns of damage, before walking towards the edge of the graveyard where it met the side wall and back garden of the neighbouring house. Harrison walked along the perimeter, head down, like a dog on a scent, until he came to the broken gate that led from the far end of the garden into the churchyard. What would have once been an easy access for the vicar from his house to place of work, was now the route for something else. Something which had created fear in the homeowner and her children – and gone on to sell more than a few newspapers with their lurid headlines.

Before he left the churchyard, Harrison walked across to the door of the church, where large grooves had been gouged into the thick wood, around three feet from the ground. They were deep, created by something with four sharp claws that had scraped at the wood, presumably attempting to get in.

Satisfied that he had seen enough of the evidence, Harrison Lane strode back down the path to where the detective stood waiting for him, a pensive but expectant look on his face.

'Is the neighbour in for me to speak to?' Harrison said to him.

'Yes, she's expecting you. Well... so what do you think?' DS Potter couldn't contain himself any longer.

'I'll explain shortly,' Harrison replied, walking off so that the slightly below average height detective had to almost jog to keep up with his six-foot-two stride.

When they knocked on the door, a sharp yapping noise preceded the sound of small, clawed feet scrambling along tiled flooring towards the front door, followed by human footsteps.

The door to the house, which was still called 'The Vicarage', was opened by a black-haired woman in her early fifties, holding a yapping dachshund. Her eyes took in the handsome muscular man on her doorstep, pupils dilating slightly to betray her first impressions.

'Mrs Harcourt, this is Dr Harrison Lane, the ritualistic crime expert I was telling you about. Susanne Harcourt,' DS Potter introduced them.

'Pleasure to meet you.' She smiled, offering her free right hand.

Harrison accepted the handshake and then offered his hand to the small dog, which quickly subsided from barking to sniffing and then licking it.

'Aww, Dezzy likes you,' Susanne said, kissing the small dog's head.

'Would it be OK if I came in and looked around your back garden?' Harrison asked.

'Absolutely, yes of course,' she replied, a little taken aback by his directness.

'How long have you lived here?' he questioned as they walked through the hallway to the kitchen and back door. Everywhere looked freshly painted and there was the smell of new carpets from the hall stairs.

'We moved in six weeks ago. Everything was fine until the boys stupidly did that Ouija board thing. I never would have let them if I'd known. You just never know what you might cause with those things. They had a friend over from school who brought it with him, and they thought it would be a great joke. I think they were bored – we've come from London where there's a bit more going on – but they promised me that they didn't do any of the damage to the headstones. They're good boys, you know. The police arrested them for vandalism at first, but it wasn't them. They just didn't realise what they were starting with that Ouija board. It's been a frightening lesson for them.'

She unlocked the back door and opened it for Harrison.

'I can't even let Dezzy out there now. He goes crazy. He knows there's something out there and at night he hears it too. We've asked the church if they'll agree to doing an exorcism. I just don't know how much longer I can stand living here like this. I'm terrified every evening. It knocked over the birdbath we brought from London last week.'

Harrison didn't reply but walked off down the garden, leaving Susanne, Dezzy, and the detective behind.

After an initial section of newly-laid patio and freshly-turfed lawn, the end of the back garden was more overgrown than the churchyard. It was long, stretching the length of the church grounds, and as Harrison neared the end, he could see it sloped down, although there were bushes across the entire area that meant it was impossible to go much further. He didn't need to though: on the ground he saw the evidence for what he'd suspected and it tallied with what he'd seen in the churchyard.

Harrison strode back to the three expectant faces.

'OK, shall we go inside?' he said. 'I know exactly what's been going on here.'

Susanne and DS Potter perched on the edge of the sofa, anxiously looking to Harrison.

'Did you do the update work on the house?' he asked as he looked around what had clearly been a recently decorated sitting-room area.

'Yes. It was pretty ramshackle when I bought it. Hadn't been lived in for a while. Do you think that's a problem? Have I disturbed something with the work? A poltergeist?'

It was highly unusual for Dr Harrison Lane to show any kind of humour in his work. He was known for his intensity, and this was still a serious situation, but he couldn't help smiling.

'Not exactly. I presume you tidied up the garden a little too?'

She nodded. 'Just the first section. I'll get the end part sorted – if I stay.'

'I suspect that there aren't many properties around here that go on the open market?' Harrison fished.

Susanne shook her head, confused at the amused look on his face.

'And if I'm not mistaken, you're recently divorced, so you're not used to living on your own, especially in the country.' In the sitting room Harrison saw photographs of a middle-aged woman who looked far more jaded than the one who now sat in front of him. This woman wore no wedding ring and had clearly spruced herself up. There were no grey hairs, he suspected filler and Botox had been used on her face, and she was fitter and slimmer than the woman in the photographs.

'Well, yes, but that's got nothing whatsoever to do with this. Are you trying to imply that it's all in my head?'

'No, no, not at all, please don't take offence. The damage is very real. What I can tell you for sure is that there is nothing paranormal in what has been going on here. What I suspect is that the locals almost certainly know that too and I've no doubt the pub I drove past in the village has been doing a roaring trade.'

'Well, yes it has as a matter of fact. Are you telling me they've set this all up, that it's the villagers doing this, trying to scare me? My boys had to be questioned at the police station. If I find out...'

'No, they've not instigated it, but I've no doubt they know what is causing it. You say Dezzy goes crazy if he goes in the garden?'

'Yes, tries to disappear off into the overgrown part at the end, it took me ages to get him back the first time he did it. I had to send the boys in after him and he'd got all tangled in some brambles. Now we know what's going on, I don't let him out there at all.'

'They were first bred in Germany; do you know what the German translation is for a dachshund?'

'Err, no. I've never studied German. They were bred for hunting foxes or something.'

'The literal translation is badger dog. Dezzy is using his natural instincts as a badger hunter. You've got a sett at the far end of your garden and they're digging tunnels under the churchyard which has caused the subsidence. I suspect that the works in your garden disturbed them and so they've dug some new tunnels. They'll also be coming around your back garden at night looking for food and they're quite clumsy and strong, so probably knocked over the birdbath.'

'Badgers! Are you serious?' DS Potter stammered.

'Absolutely.'

'What about the church door?'

'Had there been any events or services in the church prior to the scratches appearing?'

'The local primary school held a harvest festival in there,' Susanne replied. 'That was just as this was all starting up.'

'Mmmm, and I suspect that they all brought vegetables, fruit, and things to the church. The badgers have a very good sense of smell, they'd have smelt the food in the church and tried to get to it. Their front feet have long strong claws which they use for digging and can easily score those marks in a wooden door.'

'So you're saying that the locals are in on this; that they knew all along what was causing it?' The detective was clearly more annoyed and embarrassed about being one of the last to find out.

'I would hazard a guess, yes. The locals will know that there are badgers around the area. This is a very small rural community that probably doesn't want to be swamped by townsfolk pushing up house prices. They don't mind if they just visit, spending money in their businesses and disappearing back to the big smoke. They also have a disdain for people who don't understand the country. There are plenty of town dwellers who move to the countryside and then complain about the noises or smells from farm animals, or nature. You told me that they're angry about their village police station being closed and having to come under the town force. I think they're enjoying, if you don't mind me saying, your countryside ignorance. Proving a point if you like.'

DS Potter swore and then immediately apologised to Susanne.

'And, Susanne,' Harrison continued, 'it must be hard finding yourself on your own in a strange place so that has probably spooked you somewhat, aided by Dezzy's constant vigilance. The boys mucking about with the Ouija board probably helped spur on the imagination too.'

'Yes, but...' The detective shook his head.

Susanne started to giggle next to him. 'Badgers,' she said. 'Oh my God, wait until I tell the boys.'

'What am I going to tell the media? My boss?' DS Potter said to Harrison.

'I'm afraid I will leave the detail to you, but you were right about this not being caused by anything human, and you can tell him the case is solved.' Harrison turned back to Susanne. 'It should be possible to relocate the sett if you get some wildlife experts in. That way you'll be able to let Dezzy out the back door and the churchyard won't collapse into the badger tunnel network. I'd have another word with the church. Relocating badgers will be far less controversial than an exorcism.' Harrison stood up to leave.

'Thank you so much,' Susanne said, jumping up from the sofa. 'I can't tell you what a weight you have lifted from my shoulders. I've been going to bed with a crucifix every night and waking up every couple of hours to noises or Dezzy barking. I must have recited the Lord's Prayer about a thousand times.' She beamed at him and offered her hand again, which he took.

'Best of luck with your new life,' he said to her, and as he left he thought that, with her positive attitude and sense of humour, she could still make a go of her new village life. DS Potter, however, would probably never get over the humiliation.

Harrison was still smiling when he returned to his Harley Davidson, ready to head back to London. It wasn't often he got to solve a case in under an hour, but the text from his assistant, Ryan, soon wiped the smile from his face. His next case was in and wasn't going to be so simple. This time the stakes were much higher: there'd been a murder and he was needed in Yorkshire.

THREE

Ryan was just contemplating opening another packet of cheesy Wotsits when his phone rang. He looked longingly at the unopened packet, before answering the call.

'Yo, boss.' He smiled down the phone, the rude interruption of his Wotsits obsession forgiven. He'd been expecting this call.

'I'm downstairs.'

Ryan didn't have the chance to answer because Harrison ended the conversation. It didn't faze him: he was used to his boss's sparse social skills. Instead he crossed to the keypad by his flat's front door, and buzzed him in before unlocking the four bolts and locks on the door. A run-in with a dangerous gang last year meant he could never be too safe.

'Well that was a wild goose chase,' Harrison said as his big bulk came through the door. 'Or more to the point, a wild badger chase!' With his hand, he ruffled his hair where it had been flattened by his motorbike helmet.

'Badger chase?' Ryan looked quizzically at the man who was employed to solve ritualistic crimes, not do nature tours.

'Turns out the evil spirit conjured up by the teenage boys was a family of badgers. Their sett is at the bottom of their garden and the vicarage house had been empty for a number of years. When the Harcourts moved in, it must have upset the badgers and sent them digging in a different direction – underneath the churchyard, which then caused some of the graves to cave in. I'd bet the locals knew what was going on but were amused by the townies thinking it was some demon conjured up by their Ouija board.'

Ryan laughed and was grateful to see that his boss was amused by the story too.

'So, what's this about an Egyptian tomb murder in a Yorkshire cave?' Harrison got straight back down to business.

'It's just come in, but DI Bartholomew wants us to look into it ASAP.'

Detective Inspector Sebastian Bartholomew was their boss at the National Crime Agency who sent them any of the more unusual crimes that police forces were struggling to understand. He'd poached Harrison and Ryan from the London Metropolitan police, where they'd set up their Ritualistic Behavioural Crime unit, but had found themselves in demand across the country. Harrison's unorthodox childhood had led him to study for a doctorate in psychology, specialising in rituals and religion. This, combined with an obsession for catching the bad guys and helping victims thanks to the still unsolved murder of his mother, made Harrison a single-minded and very successful investigator, aided by expert tracking skills.

Badgers forgotten, Harrison tugged off his black leather motorbike jacket and flopped onto Ryan's sofa ready to go through the information they had.

'Glass of water first?' Ryan asked. He knew him so well. 'Or I've got some of your tea if you prefer?'

'Water's fine thanks. How's the diet going?' Harrison's eagle eyes didn't miss a thing. He'd spotted the empty pack of Wotsits.

'Good. I think...' Ryan tailed off. 'Not sure if I've lost any weight, but I bought the six pack of crisps so that I can have smaller portions like you suggested, rather than the family-sized bag.' Ryan walked away from his boss at this point, keen to not let him see the guilt on his face which came with the knowledge that although he had bought his snacks in small portion sizes, it didn't mean to say he only stuck to one at a time.

'Keep it up, Ryan,' Harrison said from the sofa. They'd had a big discussion about Ryan needing to get a grip on his eating habits a few weeks before. When Harrison had met him, he'd had far unhealthier habits thanks to the crowd he'd been working for, and that had transferred into a love for junk food. They were two extremes. Harrison the exercise obsessive, who loved to be outdoors, didn't drink caffeine and ate healthily, and Ryan the agoraphobic who sat at his computer all day never getting fresh air and sunlight and eating bad food. Harrison had rescued him more than once and he was determined to make sure he stayed healthy. Besides, they worked well as a team.

'Anything else that I need to look at before I head to York-shire?' Harrison asked.

'Nothing that can't wait. There's that satanic graffiti appearing on the London Underground's Northern line again, but it's the same as before.'

Harrison already had a theory about who might be behind the graffiti and had shared that with the police, but tight resourcing meant they'd not been able to follow up on it yet.

'How far away is this cave murder?'

'About four and a half hours.'

'I might head down there tonight so I can look at the scene fresh first thing tomorrow.' Outside the window, the daylight was fast disappearing. 'Might take the car if it's that far.'

Ryan didn't say anything. He wasn't a psychologist like his boss, but he knew that Harrison had been avoiding being at home too much ever since he and his girlfriend, Tanya, had decided to take some time out. Word from their friend, DS Jack

Salter, who worked with her, was that neither she nor Harrison had been particularly happy since. With a distinct lack of experience in affairs of the heart, Ryan hadn't dared interfere – so far.

'I'll need a hotel with a gym. I'll head home and pick up some stuff first.'

'Already on that, found the perfect place near to the crime scene.'

'Thanks, Ryan, so what are we looking at?'

Ryan handed Harrison his water and collected his laptop before joining him.

'Bit of history to this one,' he said, his eyes peering through his glasses at the screen. 'This morning, a group of six adults, all in their late forties, went into a small cave to allegedly meet up with another old university friend who they hadn't seen in around thirty years. They had received an invitation or letter from this friend asking them to meet him there.'

Harrison frowned.

'Yeah I know, who would want to go meet someone you hadn't seen for thirty years in a cave! But there's more to this. Thirty years ago, this same group, plus one other guy, were involved in an accident in which one of them was killed and another injured. The accident was in that same cave.'

'Why is this one for me though if it's just a caving accident?'

'Ah no, it's not like that,' Ryan pulled up some newspaper stories and turned his laptop round to show Harrison as he talked. This group, back then, were believed to be involved in some kind of ancient Egyptian satanic cult and there were all sorts of rumours about what they'd been up to in that cave prior to the accident. When the police arrived at the scene this afternoon, they found evidence of that same cult in the caves again, and the murder victim was wearing a mask of an Egyptian god.'

'What's their excuse for that then?'

'Well, they all told the same story about mysterious

growling noises, white mist and a metal spike which appeared out of nowhere and killed this old friend of theirs, but claim they know nothing about it and haven't seen each other in decades.'

'Hmm, OK.'

'I've put together some information on the occult group for you. The Temple of Set. It calls itself a new religion but was born out of the Church of Satan.'

'Ah yes, I'm familiar with them, not what I'd call a cult in British tabloid terms. They also don't have much of a presence in the UK so this could be a copycat or an offshoot doing their own thing, but we'll see. Thanks, Ryan.'

Ryan looked at the big man in front of him. It never ceased to amaze him just how much Harrison knew about the world's religions and cults, or his understanding of what drives humans to believe in them. Now his boss would be delving back into one of the world's oldest religions. Thousands of years before Christ, when Egyptian civilisation had its own gods and beliefs. This would be right up Harrison's street.

FOUR

Detective Sergeant Melinda Fallon wasn't looking forward to having to go back into the caves. She was glad that late last night they'd been able to remove the body, but nonetheless, all the Egyptian stuff gave her the creeps. It was a little before 8 a.m. and she felt like she'd only just left the place a few minutes earlier. The only difference was that now there was some daylight and the dusty dry earth of the car park area had darkened with the heavy autumn dew that soaked into its surface while she'd managed to catch a few precious hours of sleep.

It wasn't even as if she'd had a good sleep. The five hours that she'd lain in bed, willing the tiredness to send her under, had not been successful. Every time she'd closed her eyes, she'd seen the inside of the cave. The disturbing vision of the dead man and the mask he was wearing, and the creepy, crazed story she'd heard from the first responders who'd arrived to find six people in a state of shock with one of them babbling about an angry Egyptian god, spirit mists and a growling monster.

They'd had to call out armed backup, concerned that somebody could still be inside waiting to kill again. From the witness accounts, the victim was highly unlikely to still be alive and in need of medical assistance. It was only with the confidence that the firearms squad brought them, that they finally ventured inside to take a look.

This was only her second major incident as senior investigating officer. Her male colleagues seemed to have been given far more opportunities than she'd received and she knew exactly why that was. She also suspected that their boss, Detective Superintendent Julian Smith, had suggested this was given to her because of its creepy and unusual nature. It already looked like it could potentially be a really hard one to solve. The remote outdoor location, lack of CCTV and other witnesses and difficulty finding good forensic evidence, all pointed to it being a tough case. The kind of case that left a black mark on your career record. Meanwhile, the neat domestic murder that had also come in yesterday went to DS Bruce Hewitt. Some days it was tough realising that she had to work twice as hard as her male colleagues, but then the women police officers before her had had it far worse. At least now there were processes in place through which she could complain. Sadly, it just didn't alter some ingrained attitudes.

DS Fallon twisted the engagement ring round on her finger and gave a heavy sigh. Last night's poor sleep had come on top of months of bad rest; but she couldn't blame that on the job. In fact, work had been the only thing keeping her sane. She took a couple of paracetamols with the last few sips of her Americano coffee as the car of the man she'd been waiting for, came into view. The National Crime Agency had sent their ritualistic crime boffin to help with the inquiry and he'd requested that they meet up at the scene. She was glad of some expert help with all the Egyptian stuff, but she still had yet to interview all the witnesses so she hoped he wasn't going to take up too much of her time with his dusty books and irrelevant historical knowledge.

DS Fallon got out of her car and leaned against the door

while she waited for Dr Lane to park and join her. As he got out, she stood to attention subconsciously, suddenly energised by the handsome, muscular man who was now walking towards her.

'Dr Harrison Lane?' she queried, wondering if she'd totally got it wrong and this was someone else.

'Yes, DS Fallon?'

She nodded. Harrison Lane had black hair with deep brown eyes that seemed to search inside her. He was no desk boffin. Although fully clothed, she noted thick muscular arms beneath his jacket and couldn't help wondering if his six pack was as good as she was now imagining it to be. Intelligence, good looks *and* a fit body! For a moment she allowed herself to dwell on those thoughts, before glancing down again at her engagement ring and feeling the guilt. Would that ever change?

'As I said on the phone, we've removed the victim's body and I'm hoping he'll be fast-tracked for an autopsy this morning. Although cause of death was pretty obvious. We think that—'

'Sorry, but could I look at the scene first and then we can talk?' Harrison cut in. 'I've read the initial witness statements.'

'Right,' she said, feeling herself colour with embarrassment, 'yes, if that's what you'd prefer.'

She walked off up the hill quickly so that he didn't see her red cheeks. Intelligence, good looks and a fit body, but not all that great on the manners and social skills front. There's always some catch, she thought.

There was no further conversation as they walked and all DS Fallon could think about was the fact he was going to be having a great view of her backside as he walked up the hill behind her. She should have let him go first. As they reached the entrance to the cave, she gathered the confidence to speak to him again.

'The entrance was hidden, covered with brambles and the like,' she said to him.

'I can see,' Harrison replied, looking at the cut vegetation.

Smart arse too, Melinda thought to herself.

'Am I OK to go in alone?'

'Oh, you don't want me coming with you?' She couldn't help sounding surprised and was a little embarrassed again in front of the uniformed officer who was on duty to prevent anyone unauthorised going into the crime scene.

'If you don't mind, I like to view a scene alone and form my own opinions. I trust that is OK with forensics?' Harrison's voice had softened slightly. He'd clearly picked up on her discomfort.

'They've done some of the initial work, not easy in a place like that, but I think there's still a couple of them working in the end chamber where the victim was. You need to wear gloves and overshoes please, and don't touch anything.' Melinda put on her commanding voice, eager to take back control of the situation.

She nodded at the box near to where the officer stood and Harrison crossed over to it, taking out the gloves and shoes as directed. She toyed with the idea of insisting that she went in with him, following silently behind, but she knew this guy had a first-rate reputation and was highly recommended by the NCA. Besides, it meant she could stay outside in the autumn sun that was making a valiant attempt to evaporate last night's dew.

As she watched his broad shoulders disappear into the dark mouth of the cave entrance, DS Melinda Fallon's mind wandered back to thinking about his good looks and whether she could forgive him his abruptness, before the memory of what she'd seen in the far cave chamber made her shiver and focus back on the job she had been given, the near impossible task she had to find a killer.

FIVE

Harrison Lane stepped into the gloomy entrance of the cave and simply stood there a while, allowing his eyes to adjust to the dim light. Outside he could hear the low hum of the police officer talking to the detective he'd just met. He focused his mind, using his breathing to do so. Shutting out the external sounds and tuning in to the cave and its environment.

He heard the echoing drip drip of water coming from the tunnel in front of him. No birdsong made its way inside. This was another world. A world of darkness only suited to a small minority of the creatures we are used to. Spider webs stretched across the entrance, primed to catch on the faces of anyone who brushed by them, their creators waiting to pounce on the moths and midges that sought out the damp darkness. Anaemic vegetation reached for the light, their roots grounded in soft shallow soil away from competitors. The smell of damp and musty still air was all around.

Harrison tuned in to this underground world, ready to experience it as the victim and the witnesses had, and to find the evidence to prove what had really happened here.

He walked carefully into the rock tunnel ahead of him. His

height and bulk didn't ease his passage through what was at times a narrow corridor. The walls were damp and with the coolness of the dark underground world, his skin began to goose pimple. It was this physical reaction which would often start to give people psychological symptoms and set their imaginations running wild.

Speluncaphobia is the fear of caves. He could understand it. In this dark underground world, our usual waypoints and land-marks don't exist. Our brains, devoid of the usual bombardment from visual clues, has only the sounds and smells of the place to form a picture. But even the sounds can lie, echoing and bouncing off rock. So our brains are left to interpret these with a hefty dose of trepidation, causing us to go into fight or flight mode aided by claustrophobic fear.

Some claim that the microbiome of caves creates that anxi-ety. The fungal spores and bacteria in this strange dark world impacting our own chemical balance. Harrison wasn't sure if this was true or not. What he did know was that the human mind was capable of great imagination, seeing patterns and meaning in the unknown. Is this what had happened here yesterday, or was there something far more purposeful and man-made in the events that unfolded?

The initial statements of the witnesses said a white mist had followed them through the tunnel into the main chamber. One of them had suggested that it must have come from outside, but the others were cagier about that idea, one calling it a *shut*, which is the ancient Egyptian belief of a deceased person's shadow. Another saying it was otherworldly, but all of them had seen it. They'd also all heard a deep growl.

Harrison walked slowly, scanning the walls, ceiling and floor of the tunnel he walked down. He could see nothing other than rock and in the odd sections, where the tunnel was widest, the calcified stalactites hanging from the ceiling and dripping into small pools of water.

Before long, a white glow of forensic lights leached into the tunnel and soon he found himself in a large rock chamber. As before, Harrison stood still, taking in the whole scene in front of him before progressing.

Ordinarily this would have been a pretty majestic natural sight; a large cavern, with limestone, shale and sandstone. Harrison wasn't a geologist, but at a guess he'd say this particular cave was the result of a combination of nature and some basic historic mining in the area. Parts of it appeared untouched for centuries, the parts the stalactites inhabited; but in some areas there were clear sections where the walls had been hewn straight, with cut marks from man-made tools.

Today, those straight-cut cave walls had been daubed with Egyptian hieroglyphs and imagery as though the rock had been cut in order to make some kind of primitive blackboard or artist's canvas. In the centre of the cavern was a large wooden statue of the god Set. Big earthenware jars were placed around him. Harrison walked over to these, taking photographs of their contents – burnt down candles – and placing his foot in the photograph for scale. In front of the statue was a board with an inverse silver pentagram and a makeshift altar. A slaughtered rabbit, its black bead-like eyes staring blankly, lay next to incongruously bright fresh fruit, a bloodied knife, and a small hand bell. There was something else too, what at first sight looked to be a couple of brown sludges, but on closer inspection one piece appeared to have a human head, and the other legs. A wax doll but its torso was missing.

Harrison took more photographs before going to the walls and looking closely at what had been daubed on them. There were crude depictions of the Set animal, a kind of thin canine with long legs, a forked tail and the long sloping nose of an aardvark with square ears. Harrison suspected that some of the hieroglyphs were the Set name. He took photographs of them, which Ryan would forward on to a colleague who was an Egyptologist and far more converse with hieroglyphs than Harrison.

He didn't just look at the obvious; Harrison spent the next fifteen minutes scanning the floor of the cave and the walls again, searching for anything that could help explain yesterday's events. Finally, he was ready to go through into the next, smaller chamber where he knew the victim had died.

The body had been removed, but his spilled blood was more than evident on the ground in front of the back wall. Two fully suited forensics officers were kneeling on the floor a few feet from the wall, carefully brushing sand and other debris.

'Hi,' Harrison said, making one of them jump. 'I'm just taking a look around. Harrison Lane from the Ritualistic Behavioural Crime unit.'

'Hi, OK,' one of them said. 'You've got a real good 'un here. Like something out of an Indiana Jones movie.'

Harrison moved over to where they knelt and crouched down to look at what they were doing.

'So what we got, some kind of pressure pad?'

'Yup. Whoever set this up must have shifted around the shale and sand in order to embed this. The pressure pad is here, crude but effective. Once it was trodden on, it released a spring-loaded device that had a large metal spike on it; think of an upside-down mousetrap with an added bite. That went into the victim's chest. We've removed that part of the device to the lab, just freeing up whatever is involved in the trigger mechanism.'

A piece of flat wood, around three feet in length, had become visible in the sand.

'Very precise,' Harrison mused out loud. 'If they'd stepped to the sides, it wouldn't have gone off as planned.'

'No. But it's dead centre from the entrance, so the natural instinct is to walk ahead I guess,' the forensic officer said, looking from the entrance to the wall.

'Mmmm.' Harrison stood back up and walked across to the

wall, avoiding the bloodied area. Iron rings had been hammered into the rock, presumably where the victim had been tied. This whole plan would have been weeks if not months in the making.

'Do you know exactly where on the body the spike pierced?' Harrison asked the two officers.

They both shook their heads. 'You'll have to ask the SIO or pathologist for that info. Not our department,' the chatty one replied, getting back to the job in hand.

Harrison spent a few more minutes in the small chamber, looking around the walls and floor, before returning to the main chamber and the exit. As he walked out back into daylight, blinking from the sudden brightness, he saw DS Fallon on her mobile phone. She raised a hand to him as she saw him come out, and looked like she was attempting to finish the phone call. He waited.

'Yes, sir, yes... I know, sir... I will... Of course... Yes,' she was saying.

It was clearly a decidedly one-way conversation. Harrison hazarded a guess it was her boss.

Eventually she finished with a sigh and looked to Harrison.

'What do you think? We dealing with some kind of cult here?'

'I have a few ideas but I need to know more about those involved first,' Harrison replied. He never liked sharing too much without the full picture. It led to suppositions and the risk that evidence could be interpreted to fit a theory rather than a theory being developed from the facts.

DS Fallon nodded in acceptance.

'Let's get back to the incident room and you can view what we have. All the witnesses went home last night. We took initial statements but I want to interview them all in more detail.'

'This cave,' Harrison said to her back as he followed her down the hill, 'is it well known?'

'No, from what I can gather, the entrance was completely

hidden from any hikers who come along here. Obviously thirty years ago it hit the headlines, but since then I think it's slipped back into obscurity.' She turned to look up at Harrison. 'You're thinking about the amount of prep that must have gone into this?'

He nodded.

'Yeah, must have taken a lot of planning and work. I mean where did that statue come from? It certainly would have all taken a lot of effort for just one man. There were seven people here yesterday. One of them is dead and the other six say they had been invited by him and hadn't been back here in thirty years. All of them claim to have heard something or someone else in the cave with them. We could be talking about a third party who set this up. Or we could be looking at some kind of group ritual that's gone wrong. The only other possibility is some bizarre suicide, but right now I've not got any motives or explanations for any of it.' DS Fallon turned again to look at Harrison. 'I was kind of hoping you might throw some light on what all that stuff in the cave means.'

Harrison looked at the young woman in front of him. There was a sliver of desperation in her eyes and he didn't think that was just down to her being relatively inexperienced and it being the first day of a new case. Perhaps the earlier phone call was to blame.

'We'll get to the bottom of it,' he said reassuringly, but it was already obvious that this one was not going to be anywhere near as easy to solve as the badger case. Something told him this was going to be a tough one.

SIX

Harrison followed DS Fallon's car, and they arrived in the station car park about twenty minutes later. She'd driven fast, clearly in a hurry, and there'd been a couple of times he'd nearly lost her. Once they'd parked and were heading into the building, the reason for her speed became clear.

'Detective Superintendent Smith has called for a briefing in ten minutes,' she said to him. 'Wants to be kept informed of what's happening in the case.' She tried to be professional, but her tone betrayed how she felt about that.

'You reporting directly to him?' he asked, wondering why there wasn't a Detective Inspector in the mix.

'Yeah. He thinks this has the potential to become a PR nightmare and DI Chamberlain is off sick.'

'What's he like?' Harrison fished as she signed him in and the receptionist handed over a visitor pass.

'Smith? Oh, he'll be fine with you, no worries.'

Her reply told Harrison far more than the words intended.

They walked in through some double doors and the sound of a busy incident room could be heard through a door on their right.

'There's a little kitchen in there,' Fallon nodded to their left, 'toilets are straight ahead. If you don't mind, I need a few minutes just to gather myself before the briefing. We'll be meeting in that room at the end on the right. Will you be OK if I—'

'Yes of course, I'll be fine,' Harrison said. He'd get a glass of water and freshen up before the briefing himself. It was clear the DS wanted to have a few minutes of head space, and he could certainly empathise with that.

Ten minutes later, Harrison was in his favourite briefing meeting position, at the very back of the room where he could survey everyone and everything. About nine officers, a mix of uniformed, detective and forensic support staff, had filed into the room, each one giving him a curious glance, or in some cases, an admiring one.

DS Fallon slipped into the room, heading straight to the front, and about a minute later a balding man in his fifties strode in her wake. With his arrival, DS Fallon stood up and clapped her hands.

'OK, everyone, let's get started. First up I want an update on any ANPR and CCTV evidence we might have for the surrounding area.'

Harrison knew that the Automatic Number Plate Recognition cameras would be vital in establishing if the witnesses had been telling the truth about what time they'd arrived at the scene.

'That's me,' a young officer stuck his hand up. 'We have logged all the witnesses' vehicles heading along the dual carriageway at around the time they said that they were arriving. What we are now doing is looking for the victim's car. Nothing so far.'

'OK, thanks. So...' DS Fallon said turning to the screen

beside her. 'If we know that all six witnesses arrived at the time they said, and all of them allege that theirs were the only vehicles in that car park, is there any other way that the victim, and/or a possible killer, could have arrived, or accessed that cave before them? Aerial shots of the terrain seem to indicate that the path winds up the hill from the car park, past the cave entrance to the top and down the other side. What's on the other side? We need that whole area searched. That set up in the cave would have taken more than just a few visits. Any witnesses see someone or some people hanging around the hill, regularly passing by? There's a farm further down the road there, did they see anything? Check the ANPR for all our vehicles in the previous days and weeks.'

'Maybe they were meeting there regularly like they did before,' an officer in the front row suggested.

'Maybe. I want to know everything about the seven people involved. What have they been doing in the thirty years since the accident. For anyone who doesn't know, there's a report on the system of what happened. Thirty years ago, our victim and the witnesses were at Leeds University when eight of them formed a cult. They used to go to the cave at weekends and perform various rituals. They claimed it was just a bit of fun, but there was an accident. A rockfall. I believe that one of the group was killed. There were lots of rumours at the time that it was satanic, that one of their rituals went wrong and they tried to cover it up, but no charges were ever brought and the case was dropped. Why start it all up again now? All evidence of the cult was removed from the cave back then to stop it being turned into a ghoulish tourist spot and amid fears of safety. What we see there today is new.'

'Is it satanic? It looks Egyptian,' someone in the room queried.

'Good question, Josh, and that's a great opportunity to bring in our specialist. The NCA have sent us Dr Harrison Lane; he's head of the Ritualistic Behavioural Crime unit, and he's here to help us with all the mystical side of things.'

DS Fallon gestured to Harrison at the back of the room and everyone turned to look at him.

'Dr Lane, is there anything you can tell us that will help us with the inquiry? I appreciate that you've literally only just arrived and viewed the scene, but any first thoughts, such as what the statue signifies?'

'Sure,' Harrison said, and realising that it would be awkward for everyone to be twisted in their seats as he spoke, he walked down the centre to stand at the front. 'The statue is of Egyptian deity, Set, or Seth as he is sometimes also called. He had a chequered history in Egyptian religion, but he was primarily known as the god of winds, storms, chaos, war and darkness. We are talking around 3,000 years BC when he first appeared and we have images. Over time he was demonised and came to represent evil. In our more modern days certain factions believe he is the original Prince of Darkness, otherwise known as Satan, and there is historical evidence to suggest that could be true. The translations of his name in Hebrew, for example, make it highly likely he was the forebear to our modern Satan.'

A few in the room raised eyebrows, some looking at each other and pulling faces that showed their surprise at the information.

'There are some who don't see Set as evil,' Harrison continued. 'Instead that he champions individuality and helps us mere mortals by giving us a questioning mind and enabling us to achieve a higher intellect and sense of self. The Temple of Set, which was founded as a splinter group from the Church of Satan, honours him.'

'So with this Temple of Set, we're talking about some ancient Egyptian religion?' It was the Detective Superintendent who spoke now.

The others in the room listened intently to Harrison's explanation.

'Not as such, no. There was no Temple of Set in the Egyptian times, this is a modern religious movement, but it is based around the ancient Egyptian god, Set, and some of the magical beliefs that formed the basis of many religions or pagan practices that followed.'

'A cult then?'

'Well, not really, there's a great deal of misunderstanding behind that word and it creates an emotional response in people. It's not a brainwashing, closed cult like some. For example they don't worship Set as some religions do their own gods. But it does attract a certain kind of person...'

'If it's satanic, do they offer sacrifices, perhaps even human sacrifices and the like, because that's exactly what was suggested thirty years ago? Is that what this is?'

'No. That is very definitely not what Setians do and I'm not sure yet if this is what has happened here, or even if the group had anything to do with the Temple. They could just have developed their own form of religion, but I did notice certain elements in the cave that I would associate with the Temple. I need to gather more evidence first before we can definitively say one way or the other. Firstly I have to understand what form the group took thirty years ago, and what kind of people they were then and are now.'

Detective Superintendent Julian Smith sighed deeply and shook his head, then looked at the room.

'If I hear a word of this getting out into the press and discover a satanic or Egyptian media storm on my doorstep, I will find whoever is responsible and you will be reprimanded. Discretion. All of you.' He knitted his eyebrows and then looked to DS Fallon, both a warning to her and a prompt for her to carry on.

'Thank you, Dr Lane, I'm sure we'll have lots more questions for you.' She nodded her thanks to Harrison. 'Can forensics give us any preliminaries?'

A middle-aged man stood up and read from notes on his phone.

'The drawings on the cave walls are in blood. Animal, we think almost certainly rabbit. That should be confirmed today.'

'Can you tell when they were done?' DS Fallon interrupted.

'We should be able to give you some idea, obviously it won't be wholly accurate but certainly whether it's in the last forty-eight hours or months ago.'

DS Fallon nodded.

'The victim obviously suffered substantial bleeding, but we can't find any other blood around the cave system. The rabbit which was at the foot of the statue had been bled out, suggesting that maybe its blood was used for the paintings, along with others. It's obviously not an easy environment for evidence gathering. Finding DNA or fingerprints is going to be tough. We are meticulously analysing any of the items that aren't natural, such as the statue and other objects there in the hope that we can get some evidence off them, but so far there's nothing jumping out. We've also done a thorough search and found no evidence of anything that could answer where the mist came from or the growling that was reported by the witnesses.'

'Did someone check the localised weather?'

'Yes, absolutely clear day. No chance of mist or thunder at that time,' another officer responded to DS Fallon's question.

'We have taken the booby trap device that was used to kill the victim, away for testing. I'm going to be honest and say it'll be a long shot to get any DNA or fingerprints off that as it had been buried in the sand, but we'll do our best.'

He paused. 'Can I ask our expert something?'

'Of course,' Harrison said.

'I know we've mentioned the statue and the obvious penta-gram, but something else we're taking away for testing is what looks to me like a wax doll. That's Medieval witchcraft stuff, isn't it? How does that fit in?'

'Yes, I saw that and you're absolutely right, it is a wax figure, but it's the same principle as Satan. Ancient Egyptian beliefs form the foundation of most modern religions, and paganism as it came to be known, or Wicca, is one of them. Wax dolls were used by the Egyptians in a variety of ways. They were found in tombs where effigies of their deities or sometimes warriors, were put to protect the deceased in the afterlife, but they were also used in the same way we associate them being used in folklore by witches. Effigies of people were made, preferably with a personal item from the individual such as hair, or a piece of nail, and then they could be used in a magic spell or ritual to control or destroy that individual, or indeed cast a love spell on them. This practice continued into the Roman times and then on into our Pagan mythology.'

'Wow, OK, thanks. Learn something new every day in this job. We'll analyse the wax and see if that can give us any clues. Would be even better if the killer left us a nice DNA-laden fingerprint in it, or some skin.'

'Thanks, Dr Lane and Eric.' DS Fallon smiled. 'OK, I want someone tracking down anyone who knew the group thirty years ago, contact the university. Yesterday was the thirtieth anniversary of the death at the cave. It has to be connected. I particularly want the family of the student who was killed tracked down. Has someone decided to enact revenge?'

'What about the SIO who looked into that case? He might be able to help with some extra detail that couldn't go into the report,' Smith said to her. 'The case might have been dropped but as we all know, it's not always because there wasn't one to answer, just that there wasn't enough evidence to secure a conviction.'

'Yes, I'll talk to him too,' Fallon confirmed.

'Do you know who it was?'

'DI Norman.'

'Good, I know Ron, he's solid. He'll be able to give you some guidance,' Smith continued.

Harrison saw a flicker cross DS Fallon's face and guessed that 'guidance' from DI Norman wasn't top of her list of favourite things. Was she being hypersensitive or was there a real issue there? He'd soon find out.

'Anyone got anything else?'

The room stared back at her blankly.

'Let's get back to work,' she said to the team. 'Any major developments, I need to know immediately; otherwise same time tomorrow for an update.'

The Detective Superintendent left the room without another word, although Harrison saw him slapping one of the other detectives, a man in his thirties, on the back as they walked out. Harrison hung back waiting for the DS to finish talking to Eric from forensics.

'Right, I really need a coffee,' she said to Harrison after Eric had walked off. 'Can we go grab one and have a quick chat as I've got a few questions so that I can get my head around things and you can tell me what you need from us. I have to go to the mortuary in an hour, you're welcome to tag along for that if it's any use for you too?'

'Absolutely, yes. I need to review the victim.'

'That's settled then. Right, let's top up on caffeine,' she said marching out the door with purpose.

SEVEN

While DS Fallon got the drinks, Harrison texted Ryan and asked him to research the Temple of Set, particularly in this area of the UK. He knew they had regional groups that they called Pylons in the USA with some in Europe, but this was a small religion and numbers in the UK were likely even smaller. He needed to determine if this local group had anything to do with the Temple of Set, either thirty years ago or now. He also sent him some of the photographs that he'd taken earlier, with various requests for information.

'Here you go, one chamomile tea.' DS Fallon put a steaming mug in front of Harrison and placed her own black coffee down on the small café table. They'd gone to another part of the building where there was a very small canteen, which the DS reliably informed him was only open regular 8 a.m. to 5 p.m. hours and had to be supplemented by vending machines.

'We don't have long,' she started, 'but thank you again for coming to assist.' She studied his face for a few moments and Harrison could tell she was weighing up how to approach the next part of the conversation. He reached out, seeing her discomfort. There was something fragile about DS Fallon. On the outside she was tough – nothing seemed to bother her – and yet Harrison's professional psychologist eye could see a fissure in her personality that occasionally leaked vulnerability. She hid it well.

'I'm here to help. Ask me anything you want. I tend to work in partnership with the SIO on investigations like this, shadowing them so that I can get a view of the whole case. They use my specialist knowledge and combine it with detailed police work. I'll build up a picture of who our suspect is likely to be based on the crime and circumstances, and give you an insight into the kind of mind that engages in ritualistic murder, as well as explain what some of the background and history to the rituals might be.'

DS Fallon's shoulders seemed to drop in relief. 'Thanks, that's great. You can probably tell I've not come across anything like this before.'

'Most people haven't, believe me.'

She nodded.

'OK, can you just talk me through this whole Egyptian religion thing because you said in the briefing that this is relatively new and yet there's a statue of an ancient god and a booby trap like you'd get in one of the pyramid tombs. It's all totally out of place in the middle of Yorkshire.'

'OK, as I said, I'll need to talk to the witnesses, find out what form the group took originally thirty years ago. But there are some things I can tell you at the outset. Firstly, the idea that there were booby traps like in the Indiana Jones movies is completely fictional. The ancient Egyptians did try to protect the riches and most importantly the deceased's remains in the pyramids, but the kind of elaborate traps that people now associate with pyramids is pure Hollywood. That leads me to think that the method of murder was important to the killer or killers, and that could give us a good clue as to their identity going forward.'

DS Fallon was listening intently, leaning both elbows on the table and cradling her coffee as Harrison talked.

'In what way important?'

'Most killers do their work out of sight, alone. Whoever killed Jordan wanted the group to witness it, and not only that, but the method involved the group members. They were in fact the ones who effectively killed him by treading on the trip board.'

'This all keeps leading back to the group, doesn't it?' she thought out loud.

'Definitely. The Egyptian religion is more complicated. As I said in the briefing, Set was revered in ancient Egypt, but the Temple of Set – if indeed this is even related – was only established in the mid 1970s. What you have to understand is this is quite an elitist organisation. It's about seeking your true self, attaining a higher intellect and sense of yourself, or Xeper as they call it.' Harrison pronounced the latter word as 'Kheffer'. 'They don't worship Set as such, the point is self-deification with the help of Set. They aim to be far superior to all the rest of us mere mortals, achieving a god-like state and therefore eternal life.'

'Blimey, OK. Pretty serious then – they're not asking for much.'

'Yes, but Setians don't carry out human sacrifices and the like. If people don't meet their exacting standards, then they're just kicked out. It's heavily rank-orientated and initiates are expected to work hard to achieve higher status.'

'You're not convinced that this is what we have here, are you?'

'I'm honestly not sure. Same god, and from what I saw, the same methods of reaching out to him through the pentagram, but I have a few doubts about whether this was a group linked to the church. I'll reserve judgement until I know more about them.'

'But it's linked to Satanism right? As you say, there was a pentagram in there too, just like I've seen at satanic sites.'

'It was an offshoot organisation, but it's not satanic in the same way. The Church of Satan is about self-gratification and pleasure. Setians are a bit more cerebral. They believe in reincarnation and eternal life and that corrupt mere humans won't survive, that they will rise to a higher intellectual state and break the natural order becoming powerful and god-like themselves.'

'Big egos then!' the DS joked.

They both took a sip of their drinks as they thought.

Harrison looked at the young detective in front of him. She was an attractive woman, a few years his junior, brunette with minimal make-up. She was clearly ambitious and hardworking too but found time for a social life because she had a solitaire engagement ring on her left hand. For his part, he was glad he had an SIO to work with who had the right attitude.

'Can I ask you something?' Harrison queried.

She nodded.

'When the first responders entered the cave, was there any of the strange mist that the witnesses had reported?'

'No, none. You think they made that up?'

'Maybe, but not necessarily.'

'You saying it could have really been some kind of spirit?'

Harrison smiled. 'No. There is a rational explanation for everything. It was perhaps a theatrical trick to create a psychological reaction. Why, and who did it, again I'm not sure. Neither can I yet explain how, but if they are telling the truth then that gives us more clues as to the motive and killer.'

'And the growling?'

'Same.'

DS Fallon nodded again thoughtfully. 'So what we really need to do is go talk to those witnesses and try to get inside their heads now and thirty years ago.'

'Indeed.'

'But first, I'm afraid we have an appointment with the victim. I can drive us if you like, save taking two cars.'

Harrison Lane found himself in the passenger seat of DS Fallon's car, and quickly realised that the speedy driving earlier hadn't just been a symptom of rushing to get to a meeting. It didn't bother him; she was totally in command and he suspected that she enjoyed it. An area of her life where she could have complete control. She seemed oblivious to the rally-like nature of her driving skills and any potential impact on her passengers.

The pathologist was a middle-aged woman who introduced herself as Betty. Petite and efficient with short, grey, bobbed hair, she had them gathered around the unfortunate Jordan Oaks within minutes.

'Jordan John Oaks, forty-nine years of age, and until yesterday with no major medical issues. As you can see from the whopping great big hole in his chest, that was the cause of death.' Betty recounted Jordan's vital statistics in a somewhat cheery tone, as though she was reading out a weather report.

Harrison was impressed with DS Fallon's stomach. This was a particularly gory cadaver and he knew more than a few strapping blokes who wouldn't have been able to keep it together. The only tell of anything upsetting her was that she had started to twist the engagement ring on her finger.

'He didn't like being tied up,' Betty continued, 'must have known what was coming, because you'll see from the state of his wrists and ankles that he'd tried very hard to get out of the handcuffs which held him. Unfortunately for him, they'd just got tighter and nearly went through to the bone in places.' Betty pointed to Jordan's right wrist. 'I'd say he was held for more than twenty-four hours like this. He was dehydrated and there was no recent food in his stomach.'

'You mean he could have been hanging off that cave wall for all that time?' DS Fallon looked at the man's mortal remains with sympathy.

'I'm afraid so. If you come over here, I've got more to show you.' She beckoned them over to the side where steel cupboards ran along the wall and there were several metal trays on top.

'This is the mask which had been on his head at the time of death,' she said, flourishingly presenting the mask.

'That's Set again, isn't it?' DS Fallon looked to Harrison.

'It is. Strange.'

'Strange?'

'Well, if you worship or honour a god, you don't then kill their proxy,' Harrison mused aloud.

'There's something else you'll find interesting,' Betty said to them, stepping back and revealing a leather thong with a large ball of leather in the middle. 'He was gagged. You couldn't see it until the mask was taken off.'

'So how did he shout for help? They all say they heard it!' DS Fallon exclaimed.

'You tell me, because I can assure you, he wasn't capable of it at the time of death, so either somebody was there in that chamber with him and gagged him just before they came through, or it wasn't him shouting for help.'

'Or they lied.'

'Yes. There was something in his trouser pocket too,' Betty continued, pulling another tray across so that they could both peer at what was in it.

'An ankh,' Harrison exclaimed.

'What's that?' DS Fallon looked quizzically at what appeared to be a broken cross with the top a loop rather than a single stem. It had been snapped in half.

'The symbol of eternal life in ancient Egypt, the gods were often depicted carrying it. The predecessor to the Christian cross. Any idea if it was broken before his death?'

'Not possible to say I'm afraid. It was in two pieces in a pocket. It could have been damaged in the impact but you'd need to get the forensic team to work out whether that was possible with the device.'

'If it was broken before he died?' DS Fallon narrowed her eyes and looked to Harrison.

'Again, symbolic. As it's the symbol of eternal life, by breaking it the killer was sending a message that they didn't want the victim to achieve it. The injury to his chest, was it in the centre?' he asked Betty.

'Actually no, it was slightly off centre, went straight through his heart. Took out a bit more on either side mind, but the heart was pulped.'

Harrison nodded thoughtfully. 'The heart was a very important organ in Egyptian times. It was carefully taken out of the body and mummified so that it could be preserved for the deceased's reincarnation and eternal life. Seems to me that the killer was making absolutely sure that Jordan stayed earth bound.'

EIGHT

Ellie Robertson was exhausted. They were supposed to have gone to Mike's sister's for lunch but she just hadn't been up to it. She'd told him to go, rather than them both miss out, and if she was honest, she was annoyed with him anyway and didn't want to be in the same room as him for a while. When she'd finally got back from Yorkshire, late last night, breaking down in tears and telling him the story of what had happened in the cave, Mike hadn't reacted in quite the way she'd hoped.

First of all he'd been sympathetic and said she must have had a huge shock, but then he admitted that he thought she must have imagined some of it. The mist, the growling, the spike that came out of nowhere.

'So how do you explain that he's dead then!' she'd screamed at him, completely incredulous that anyone could be so insensitive.

'Calm down,' he'd said to her in his irritating soothing voice which was about as calming as pouring water on an oil fire.

Didn't people realise that saying 'calm down' to someone who was upset was a guarantee to make them more annoyed?

'All I'm saying is that in the darkness of the cave, underground in a creepy place, your imagination would have gone wild. Couldn't the mist have just been smoke from the candles?'

When she'd carried on arguing with him, he'd simply retorted, 'Well why did you go there in the first place? You've not seen him in thirty years, you get an invite and drop every-thing. Didn't you think it was a bit weird?'

He had a point with that, but there were some things about her past that Mike didn't know, and she didn't want him finding out. Instead she'd flounced off to the spare room and slammed the door shut. The neighbours would probably have heard every word.

Why did she go? She'd asked herself that a hundred times on the drive home. Because she was curious? His invitation had more than hinted at some kind of revelation about what had happened there thirty years ago. Or because she'd had an infat-uation with Jordan Oaks from the day that she had met him at Leeds, and something still burnt inside of her. What on earth she expected she didn't know, but there had been a tiny part of her which hoped that maybe, just maybe, Jordan had invited her because he too had thought about her over the years and decided to ensure he had no regrets. That, somehow, he would totally fall in love with her and they'd be consumed by passion, two soulmates together at last in the place where her immature love for him had flourished. Totally impractical and illogical of course, but maybe Mike had sensed that was the way she felt. Maybe that was why he was less than totally sympathetic. Maybe that was why she was so beside herself crying. The happy reunion with the man she'd always held a flame for, ended up in him brutally dying.

Inevitably she didn't get much rest, even if she hadn't had to contend with Mike's snoring. Horrible nightmares crashed around her head, waking her with their ferocity and making her cry out in her sleep. At one point, Mike put his head around the door, his concern overriding his annoyance. In the morning they'd been civil, although a tad frosty, and he'd offered to stay at home with her if she was still upset.

'No, your sister will be disappointed if you don't go, and your mum will be expecting you. You go, I'll be fine. Just send my apologies.'

That had been two hours ago. For the first hour she'd kept herself busy in the flat, cleaning and tidying until there was nothing more to do apart from keep moving things around. Being alone with the vivid images in her head was sending her crazy, so she'd gone for a walk.

Getting outside in the autumn sun helped. She headed straight for the park and made herself focus on nature; isn't that what the doctors say is the way to get over trauma? She listened to the birdsong in the trees and looked up into the canopy. The colours of autumn were in full show; reds, yellows and browns mixed with the evergreen. She kicked at the brittle fallen leaves on the ground and memories of childhood stirred with their scent. Cosy snippets of bonfires and family walks.

Yesterday became a dream. Some terrible nightmare she'd had that wasn't true. She'd left all that behind her thirty years ago and it was just a tiny blip in her life that she could forget about and move on. There'd be more interviews with the police, no doubt. But she could shut those out. Pretend like it had never happened. She never wanted to see any of the others ever again. Never wanted to have anything more to do with them. She'd built herself a good life and she intended to get on with it. Jordan and the rest of them were parked in the past.

There'd been more of a spring in her step as she'd walked home. She could understand why Mike found it all unbeliev-able: it was. And, she was stupid to have agreed to go in the first place. She'd draw a line under it. Make up with Mike when he came home and lay her fantasy about Jordan Oaks to rest. Tonight she'd go back to their marital bed and let Mike know that she was sorry.

When she reached the flat, Amazon had delivered a parcel which one of her neighbours must have put outside their door rather than leave it downstairs where it risked going missing. There'd been a spate of porch pirates stealing parcels in the past few weeks. She picked it up thinking it was for Mike, but it was addressed to her. It was quite heavy and she rattled it. Perhaps the shock of yesterday had made her forget what she'd ordered because she just couldn't think what it was.

Ellie carried the parcel into the kitchen, putting it on the work surface while she took off her shoes and coat. Then she got some scissors out of the drawer and sliced the tape on the box. She hoped it was going to be something nice that she'd ordered herself as a treat and not some household necessity she'd bought absent-mindedly one evening or got on subscription.

Tape sliced, she opened the lid to see the usual brown paper filler packaging crumpled up inside and forming a layer over whatever the contents were. She put both hands in to pull it out.

That's when she felt the first stab of pain in her right hand. She squealed, jumping back slightly and pulling both her hands out from the box.

Attached to her right hand was a snake. A live snake with its dead black eyes, that had stuck its fangs deep into the flesh around her thumb.

She screamed again and began trying to shake the snake off. As she flapped her hands around, she caught a sudden movement in the corner of her eye and a second snake launched out from underneath the brown paper in the box and bit her arm. She carried on screaming and flapping both her arms and the dark brown snakes dropped to the floor.

But they didn't just lie there or slither away. Both of them reared up, their neck hoods extended and they launched at her legs, biting repeatedly. She was backed into the corner of the kitchen, kicking at them, nowhere to escape to except past the snakes.

Her hesitation was her downfall.

If she'd had the lucidity and the calmness of mind, she would have pulled herself up onto the counter and got past them that way. But she didn't. She panicked.

Ellie tried to jump over the snakes, just as a sudden pain in her abdomen caused her to retch, and so she stumbled, almost falling onto the already irritated and aggressive reptiles.

Her mobile. Where was her mobile? She couldn't see it. If she could call for help, she'd be OK.

It had been in her jacket pocket on the walk. She must have left it in there, distracted by the parcel.

Ellie staggered to the hall cupboard where the coats hung, her vision becoming blurred. She'd no idea how many bites she'd sustained, but she knew they were cobras and that meant they were highly poisonous. That poison was now coursing through her veins, and her body and brain was starting to shut down.

She retched again, her breath becoming shallow and fast. Panic and fear had already increased her heart rate, but now the poison added its effect. The faster her heart raced, the quicker the toxin was spread around her system.

She had to get her mobile.

Her hand reached into the pocket of the jacket she'd been wearing. It wasn't there. She tried the other one. Empty again.

No. It had to be there. She fumbled around frantically in both pockets again before turning round to look back towards the kitchen.

There it was, on the countertop behind the parcel box. It had been there all along.

Ellie stumbled towards it, not caring about the snakes anymore; they'd done their worst. If she didn't get help very soon, she knew it would be too late.

She lurched at the countertop, just reaching her mobile, but her breathing was getting more laboured and she felt herself dip in and out of consciousness.

She slumped a moment, hitting her chin on the counter and biting her tongue. She didn't even feel it. All she could think about was calling for help. She hung on to the kitchen top by her elbows, peering at her phone which seemed to swing and blur in front of her, and she attempted to dial the emergency services.

There was no time to think why or who had done this to her, just the desperate need to get help. The whirring in her ears grew louder before she finally blacked out.

Her mobile phone tipped from her hand onto the kitchen floor, the emergency number only partially dialled, and seconds later she joined it with a loud thud and crack.

NINE

The wax figure bubbled and melted in front of them as the flames licked at its brown globular mess. It had been easy to get a hair from Ellie and add it to the doll to make sure the magic was more powerful. Getting the snakes had been a lot harder, but if there was one thing that they'd learned in life, it was that where there's a will, there's a way. That and a bit of dark web exploration and a not inconsiderable amount of digital currency.

The euphoria from yesterday was still coursing through their blood. The terror on Jordan's face. The fear and surprise from the rest of the group. It had been perfect. Everything had gone to plan.

By now Ellie Robertson was probably dead, or at least very nearly dead. There was no doubt in their mind that the plan would work. No doubt that success would be theirs.

It had been a long time coming, and it would be sweet.

Two down.

TEN

After the autopsy, DS Fallon and Harrison Lane drove straight to Jordan Oaks's residence, a forty-five-minute drive south.

'He's never married,' the DS informed Harrison on the way. 'Lived alone. Had a reasonably well-paid job in middle management and had kept his nose clean for the last thirty years. That's pretty much all we know about him. But it was Jordan who invited all the others to the cave yesterday. I'm hoping we might get a clue as to why.'

Jordan's house turned out to be a recent build detached property on a nice estate where every house had a garage and an extra parking space, and there were speed bumps in the road to keep the residents and their offspring safe.

'We've still not found Jordan's car, or worked out how he got to the cave,' the DS told Harrison as they pulled up next to a marked police car. 'We had to get a locksmith in to gain entrance as there were no keys or other possessions on the body; but nobody's been inside yet. We'll need to be fully suited.'

Harrison knew that DS Fallon wasn't expecting him to put on his best work blazer, but was referring to the forensic over-suits, shoes and gloves they needed to wear in order not to contaminate a scene. He hoped that she'd got a good selection of sizes in the boot of her car and hadn't just brought ones that would fit her.

'You should find something your size,' she said to him as she opened up the trunk, and he breathed a sigh of relief at a neatly ordered selection of forensic wear, including an XL to cover his tall bulk.

Harrison held back and allowed DS Fallon to go inside first. She'd turned to look at him quizzically, but then must have remembered his request earlier that morning to look around alone and moved on to conduct her search.

Understanding the victim was a really important element in solving a murder. Why had Jordan Oaks been targeted, and equally critically, why had he invited the others there yesterday?

Every house displays clues about its owner or owners. Not just in the style of furniture and decoration, but in the smell of the place, the food in the cupboards, the books on the shelves. DS Fallon would be looking for a smoking gun. Evidence. Something tangible which clearly linked Jordan to the events of yesterday. Harrison wanted to find the more subtle aspects which could give him a personal insight into Jordan's character.

The first thing that hit Harrison, especially after the mortuary, was that the house smelled clean. Jordan clearly looked after the place: this wasn't a beer-loving bachelor's pad. The hallway was small and characterless, so Harrison turned into the doorway that led through to the sitting room and had his first revelation about the man.

The room was beautifully decorated with scatter cushions and pot plants, along with some expensive-looking wallpaper. The walls had a sage green and gold scene of peacocks in a garden, the kind of opulent imagery you'd find in a stately home. On the main wall there was also a large black and white photograph of the back of a naked man which took pride of place in the centre. An expensive television dominated the other side of the room and there was a closed laptop on the coffee table. They'd be taking that laptop back to the incident room with them so that the digital forensics team could take a look.

A small gilt bookcase was filled with novels like *The Heart's Invisible Furies* by John Boyne mixed with non-fiction titles like *Straight Jacket* by Matthew Todd and several fitness and diet books. A photograph of an older couple, presumably Jordan's parents, was in a silver frame on top. There were no religious or anti-religious books or icons anywhere.

Harrison heard DS Fallon's soft footsteps going up the stairs and as he'd finished looking in the sitting room, he walked through to the kitchen. It too was immaculate, clean and organised. He pulled open the dishwasher door and saw it was half filled. The smell wasn't too bad so the dishes weren't days old. He'd been here sometime in the last forty-eight hours. A bin, with various compartments for recycling and rubbish, sat next to the dishwasher. It too was clean, no spills, no odour of long past meals and containers. Jordan washed all his recycling before disposing of it.

Another door led presumably to the garage and Harrison took a look. Inside was a silver Audi. The car was immaculate apart from a thin layer of dust from the track which led to the car park by the cave, like Harrison had noticed on his car and that of DS Fallon's. It would suggest that Jordan had driven there at some point, but how had the car returned to the garage when its owner never made it home? Forensics would comb the car for any clues because it raised the suggestion that the killer had driven it back.

He took a walk around the garage, to see if there was anything of interest. Some wooden shelving on one side held the usual car-related items such as washer fluid and coolant, plus a robotic lawnmower; one of those oblong-shaped machines that looked as though somebody had forgotten to put the handle on it and which busied itself trimming the grass while you put your feet up on the sun lounger.

Finding nothing else of note, Harrison returned to the kitchen and looked out the window. The garden, not surprisingly, was lawned with what were usually flower-filled borders, had it not been autumn. Some yellow winter jasmine gave the garden a lick of colour along with the rusty reds of an ornamental autumn ivy which climbed along a wooden fence down one side. At the bottom he could see a wooden painted shed and, to the side of it, where somebody had brushed up leaves. Closest to the house was a small, seated area and patio with a chiminea. The garden was neat, self-contained, and controlled.

Harrison unlocked the back door and walked down to look in the shed. Just because Jordan didn't have anything on show in the house which might indicate a continued interest in the occult, didn't mean that he didn't have it hidden away. The shed was alarmed, undoubtedly the result of having been broken into in the past as Harrison could see evidence of splintered wood where the door had at one time been forced. It meant he was left with the only option of peering through the small window using his phone torch. The sight of garden tools and a bag of compost were all that stared back at him.

Back in the kitchen, the cupboards held no surprises. Jordan clearly liked his sushi and noodles. The fridge was likewise kitted out with the addition of Greek yoghurt and kimchi. It was always sad to view a victim's house like this. Life in stasis, frozen in time to never be restarted. No more than forty-eight hours ago, Jordan had been moving around his home, planning and cooking meals, perhaps entertaining friends, following a routine for work, and that was now all over. He was gone, and one day soon someone else would be living here instead.

The downstairs toilet gave Harrison some more insights into Jordan's lifestyle. There were photographs of him at Pride marches, rainbow-painted face, eyes bright with celebration. A couple of images of him with various male friends and with a little girl who looked around four in one photograph and about ten in another. Could be a godchild, Harrison thought, as he didn't think there were any siblings and therefore nieces; and they certainly didn't have a record of a child.

Harrison climbed the stairs and heard DS Fallon opening drawers in one of the rooms. He took another door, finding himself in the bathroom where a mirrored wall reflected back on him as he looked at the electric toothbrush and shaver sitting on the side. A glass walk-in shower cubicle took up around a third of the space and there was a bidet in the corner.

The spare room had been turned into a gym. There were free weights, a running machine and exercise bike, plus a yoga mat laid out on the floor by another full-length mirror.

Finally, Harrison crossed to Jordan's main bedroom which had by now been vacated by DS Fallon. It was the same as the rest of the house: neat, ordered, and clean. He did the same as he'd heard DS Fallon doing – opened drawers to look at what they contained, lifted folded tops and jumpers to check there was nothing hidden underneath. He checked under the bed, searched through the wardrobe, double-checked for secret hiding places – nothing. There was nothing to indicate that Jordan was still actively involved in any new religions or cults. Nothing to suggest he had a need in his life for any alternative religions. The man seemed to have had control of who he was and how he lived his life. He clearly had a social life and a good job. There was no evidence of medications to suggest either a physical or mental illness, no evidence that he had been disturbed or attacked before leaving his home.

'Harrison!' DS Fallon called from downstairs interrupting his thoughts. 'Take a look at this,' she shouted up.

He was done up here, and so went down to see what she'd found.

DS Fallon raised her eyebrows and handed him an evidence bag with a typewritten envelope and a black piece of card inside. The card was an invitation for Jordan to go to the cave for a thirtieth celebration of their group, as there was something really important that he needed to see. The date was two days ago. The day before the rest of the group turned up. The invitation was from Phil Stevenson.

Harrison didn't need to voice his thoughts because he knew exactly who they were going to be visiting next.

ELEVEN

'Phil Stevenson told us he'd received an invitation from Jordan, same as all the others,' DS Fallon said as she drove them to his house. 'So either he's lying, or someone else sent everyone their invites and just used the group's names.'

By now, Harrison had realised that she liked to brainstorm out loud and he wasn't always expected to answer, which was good because chatting wasn't his forte. He looked at the young brunette officer by his side. In some ways she reminded him of Tanya. Just a bit younger and slightly more edgy. He felt his insides twist at the thought of Tanya and his mind drifted to wondering what she was doing, and how she was doing. He missed her touch.

'He didn't look as though he was into any funny business, did he?' DS Fallon continued.

Harrison gave a small smile inside, 'funny business' was his friend Jack Salter's name for ritualistic or unusual religions.

'So tell me, what kind of person is it that is attracted to these new religions, or is there not a type?'

He realised he was expected to answer this one and was

more than happy to as it was his area of expertise and it pulled him out of his melancholy thoughts.

'Generally speaking, these new religious groups attract people who feel deprived in status and control. That can be economically, socially, emotionally, or physically. These kinds of religions offer them the promise of power, to rise above the rest of society – all those who look down on them. Inside the group there is also often a status hierarchy, and what you do outside in the real world is unimportant. Even cults, where there is a controlling leader, still offer that status because by believing in what they see as the real truth spoken by their prophet, they are more intelligent and knowing than all the rest of us who don't believe. They also usually offer the ultimate reward of eternal salvation while those of us on the outside are destined for annihilation.'

'Nice!' DS Fallon remarked, listening and concentrating on driving at the same time.

'Sometimes, these new religions, like the Temple of Set, preach individualism and self-worth through your own efforts, and that attracts those who blame traditional religions for a lot of the world's problems and the 'sheep' mentality they might invoke. These individuals believe their intention, or that of a supporting deity, can bring about power and change. For all of these cults and religions, within the group structure those views are validated and amplified. Their feelings of loneliness and isolation are eased by having a common view and cause, and also by the knowledge that they have their deity to support them. It brings superiority and it brings order to their world.'

'Hmmm,' DS Fallon said in response. 'Sounds like social media algorithms. The more you read lies, the more you're fed them and get connected with others with the same outlook until it seems like that's the dominant world view.'

'Well, you have a good point there,' Harrison agreed and thought that was an insightful comment.

'But don't they notice when their magic spells or prayers don't work?'

'Ah, therein lies the conundrum of all religions, myths, and conspiracy theories. You could ask that of any one of them. A believer will choose to focus on those successes which validate what they want to validate, and find excuses as to why other things didn't go as planned. The devil is and has always been a convenient scapegoat – although not the only one, the *establishment* is another. You see that throughout religions. And the thing is, that by having these beliefs, it often makes them feel better, gives them greater confidence, and so to them it ultimately works and is real.'

'So we're looking for somebody who has no control over their everyday life, or an aspect of it, and wants to feel superior to us every-day folk?'

'Maybe, if we are looking for a new religion member,' Harrison replied, 'but that really is a big if here, because the killer might have another motive and not believe in any of that.'

'What you mean the usual: money, love, revenge and the like? So why bother with all that Set stuff?'

'It could be smoke and mirrors,' Harrison said, 'or it could be that the killer wants to ridicule them or use their own beliefs against them. It would explain why Jordan was wearing the Set mask when he was killed. The more I see, the more I think that the key most certainly lies with what happened to or in this group thirty years ago.'

'Definitely, I agree, so let's see if Phil Stevenson can enlighten us any.'

Phil Stevenson was at home with his family when Harrison and DS Fallon arrived. Their home was a faux Regency-style house with a columned porch and a Mercedes out front. Inside, twin boys, aged around seven, were tearing around with fighter jets held above their heads, making jet-like noises as only seven year olds could.

It made Harrison think about the conversation that he and Tanya had, just before their trial separation. She'd asked him if he wanted children and he really wasn't sure that he did. He hadn't been sure he could make any real commitment at all, and that was the problem. His problem. The last few weeks he'd been trying to work through it. He knew it stemmed from his childhood, from the murder of his mother, but the harder part had been coming to terms with the fact he also knew it was fear. It was simpler being alone because you never had to face the possible pain of losing someone. He'd barely admitted that to himself though, let alone anyone else yet. It was no surprise therefore that their trial separation had turned out to be a prolonged period of absence.

'Gayle, why don't you take the kids to the park?' Phil Stevenson had called to his wife as soon as he saw who was at the door. They'd obviously already discussed this tactic as she didn't query it and within ten minutes the house had fallen silent.

DS Fallon and Harrison were both sat on a sofa nursing a hot cup of Yorkshire tea and a glass of water, respectively.

'Thank you for agreeing to see us again, Mr Stevenson,' the DS began. 'I want to caution you that anything you say to us could be used as evidence, but we aren't formally interviewing you at this stage.'

'Well yeah, fine of course. It's not like I'm a suspect or anything, we were just witnesses,' Phil answered, looking a little bemused at Harrison, as though Fallon didn't know what she was saying.

He was in his late forties, with grey splashes around his temples which gave him that distinguished look of middle age. For all his bravado and outward confidence, Harrison could see Phil Stevenson was not as confident and chilled as he'd like to portray. His hands kept fidgeting and he had to wipe the sweat from his palms onto his thighs, more than once. Harrison let the DS lead the questioning while he observed.

'If you don't mind, Mr Stevenson, I'd like you to start by telling us how your group got together thirty years ago.'

'Sure. We were all students at Leeds. Different courses, but somehow we all ended up in the same halls of residence and kind of hit it off.' He paused and looked at them both under his eyebrows. 'Look, we weren't the cool kids. Each of us had our own demon, whether it was crushingly low confidence or shitty upbringings. You know what it's like at that age, you're still searching for who you are and what trail you're going to follow in life. We were all thrown together and found some common ground, I guess because we understood each other.'

'And yet you all say that none of you have kept in contact at all over the past thirty years?' DS Fallon pressed. 'Not lifelong friends then? I'd have thought you'd have at least sent each other Christmas cards.'

'No.' Phil looked down at his lap and pulled a face of resigned acceptance, rubbing at his thumb and fingers.

'OK, but you formed some sort of religious group together back then?'

'Yeah, but I don't think I saw it as a religion as such. It was Jordan's idea. Someone he knew at home gave him a book and some information about an American group and he suggested we form our own.'

'What was the group and book?' Harrison asked now.

'The Temple of Set,' Phil replied looking directly at him. 'I can't remember the name of the book now.'

'Was it *The Book of Coming Forth by Night* by Michael Aquino?'

'Sounds about right, yeah.'

'You said Jordan decided to create your own group, did you not contact the Temple at all?'

Phil shook his head. 'No, there was money involved if we all had to join up and we were students with limited budgets.'

'What about the person who'd given Jordan this information, do you know what their name is?' DS Fallon asked, her pen poised over a notebook.

Phil shook his head. 'Never met the bloke and it was thirty years ago. I forget my kids names sometimes, let alone some random guy I didn't know decades ago. Besides I don't think Jordan ever even told us his name.'

'But it was a man.'

'It was a male, yes, not sure how old they were. We were only nineteen at the time. I think this person had befriended Jordan at home, helped him out mentally – you know!'

'So Jordan decided to share his newfound confidence with you all, that it?'

'Yeah. Yeah, I guess that was it.'

'What about the cave, how did it come about that you started meeting there?'

'That was Kelly. She was kind of the second-in-command, if you like. Totally embraced Jordan's group idea. Her folks didn't live too far away and she'd taken their dog for a walk around that hill some time before she started uni. The dog chased a rabbit and disappeared and so she went hunting for it and discovered the hidden cave entrance behind some bushes and stuff. It was exciting going there.' Phil smiled as he reminisced. 'Felt clandestine and risky. Going to the cave rather than staying in halls just gave the whole thing more of a mystical feel, and we were worried that someone would come into the flat and see what we were doing and misinterpret it.'

'Misinterpret it? So what did you do in this new religion?'

'Well we took the ideas from the information that Jordan had. It was all about attaining a higher intellect, finding our true selves. You can see this was pretty appealing to undergraduates who were a bit lost in life. If I remember rightly, it was the

Crystal Tablet of Set that was the first-degree membership. We worked through all the reading and did some of the magic. It was nothing terrible. We weren't sacrificing babies or having drug-fuelled orgies. We didn't even drink because it detracts from personal power and control. It was all pretty tame really but it was a bit of fun for a while.'

'So what kind of magic was it then?' DS Fallon asked.

Phil paused, thinking. 'Don't remember, much. It was just words mostly and candles, you know.' He looked at the DS and shrugged.

'Well, no actually I don't. You must remember what you did in that cave?'

'Not really, no. It was thirty years ago. I was nineteen.' Phil jutted out his chin, signalling he wasn't going to budge on his answer.

'OK, well, did it work?' DC Fallon asked.

'Work? What do you mean?'

'Did you increase your intellect? Find yourselves? You seem to have done alright?' DS Fallon waved a hand to indicate the house.

'Hard work, detective.' Phil frowned, his voice becoming terser. 'I found our little foray into an alternative religion interesting, but like I said, it was just a bit of fun.'

Harrison noticed that Phil Stevenson almost shrank down into the chair when she asked him this question. A sense of shame or defeat perhaps? Was his faux Regency house a reflection of his whole life?

'How long did it go on for?' DS Fallon continued.

Phil shrugged again, this time looking to the ceiling for inspiration. 'Oh, I don't know, a few months, maybe, most of that first year.'

'Did everything stop after the accident?'

Phil nodded sadly.

'Yeah. Morgan was killed and Andy injured. Morgan's

family totally blamed us, said we'd dragged him into a cult. The media got hold of it and started printing stories that we'd sacrificed Morgan to Set and then tried to cover it up with the rockfall. Police didn't exactly help the situation,' he added more pointedly.

'Did you?'

Phil Stevenson jumped up from his chair. 'For F—' He stopped himself from swearing, just remembering in time who he was talking to. 'I thought this was all about yesterday. I knew this would all get dragged up again. No we weren't sacrificing Morgan. There was a rockfall plain and simple. And I had absolutely nothing to do with what happened yesterday. All I did was answer an invitation and that was that. Bloody well wish I'd not been stupid enough to go.' He huffed and paced up and down the living room.

'Please sit down. Mr Stevenson, nobody is accusing you of anything. I'm just trying to understand the situation, that's all.'

Harrison was impressed with her interviewing style. DS Fallon could be kind and gentle when she wanted, and also knew just how to press the buttons to test people.

'So, you received an invitation from Jordan?'

'Yes, yes, I've told you all this.'

'Where is that invitation?'

'On the table over here.' Phil crossed the room and came back with a black invitation, exactly the same as the one they'd seen at Jordan's house, only this one said it was from Jordan.

'You'd not seen Jordan in thirty years, is that right?'

'That's right. After the accident, we went our separate ways. It was a pretty traumatic time.'

'And yet you were prepared to go back to the scene of that accident and meet up with him thirty years on.'

'Yes. No laws against reunions are there? We'd once had a bond, been close. He was also quite charismatic in his own way.

Our leader. Maybe something of our old friendship still remained and time heals, right?'

'Are you OK if we keep this?' she asked, pulling out an evidence bag for the invite.

Phil nodded.

'Talk us through what happened yesterday.'

Phil sighed. 'I arrived at the car park just before the time on the invite. It's a few minutes' walk up the hill to the cave as I'm sure you know. When I got there, Kelly was already parked and all the others arrived as we were talking. We quickly realised that we'd all been sent invites from Jordan. It said to go to the cave, so we started climbing up the hill, presuming Jordan was going to meet us.'

Neither Harrison nor DS Fallon interrupted, letting Phil do the talking.

'We went in; I think I was first in. Some of the others are a bit drippy at times, you know, they need a leader. And we started walking towards the main chamber. I could see the candlelight. Just as we reached it, there was a growl behind us, and we saw white mist coming out of the tunnel.'

He looked from one to the other of them.

'I know it sounds crazy, but I promise you it's true. It spooked us all – I'm not going to lie, I was scared. That and all the stuff on the walls and the statue, it was like stepping back in time. There was no sign of Jordan and I thought maybe he was playing some kind of sick joke so I was about to leave. That's when we heard him calling for help. We went into the smaller chamber and there he was, tied to that back wall. It was all totally overwhelming; I think we all just wanted to run but we couldn't leave him like that. So, we stepped forward to help and that's when the floor just blew up and the metal thing went through him. After that I don't remember much except we were all running, the girls screaming and then as soon as we were out, I called for help. Still hard to fathom...'

DS Fallon gave him a few moments. He was staring at the floor with a dazed expression, the shock still evident and raw after recounting the events.

Harrison looked to her to indicate he wanted to ask some questions and she gave him a small nod.

'Mr Stevenson, can I ask whether one of the group suggested it was a growling sound you heard or if you heard it independently?'

'Oh I heard it alright. It was a deep growl for sure. We all heard it. I don't think anyone specifically said it was a growl, we were just worried about what it was.'

'And the mist, that wasn't evident at all as you were walking through the tunnel, but started almost immediately after?'

'Yeah. It was like it was following us.'

'And if you don't mind me asking, you said you all had demons, that's what drew you together, so what was your demon thirty years ago? What made you want to join this group?'

Phil paused a few moments, looking at him, clearly deciding whether or not he should share. Then he took a big breath.

'My dad. He had very high expectations and could be a total shit. I never felt like I would be able to make him proud and do anything right. He's dead now, and I don't think I ever did.' The last part was said almost as a challenge to an invisible person in the room.

Harrison acknowledged the man's pain. 'Did you carry on with asking Set for help with your life?'

'No. Gayle is Roman Catholic. We take the boys to church now. Not every week, but Easter and Christmas, you know. The accident ended all that nonsense. As I said, it was a bit of student fun, it wasn't like I really believed it.'

Just then, DS Fallon's mobile phone buzzed in her pocket to indicate a call for the third time in as many minutes.

'I'm sorry would you excuse me I think someone is trying to

get hold of me,' she said to them both, standing up and walking towards the window to take the call with her back turned to them.

'Were any of the group romantically involved thirty years ago?' Harrison asked Phil.

'No. I think there were a few crushes going on. I know Ellie worshipped Jordan, but he never seemed interested in her or anyone. Do you know if he ever got married? I need to get a Facebook account like my wife and then I can stalk all my old friends and acquaintances and see how they've turned out.' Phil then looked at Harrison slightly panicked. 'When I mean stalk, I don't mean really stalk, you know I just mean see what they're up to.'

'Yes. I know,' Harrison reassured him. 'No other crushes?'

'Andy liked Paige, but she also liked Jordan. He was a good-looking guy, always had some admirer.'

'And did Jordan ever have a partner that you knew of?'

Phil shook his head. 'Strange really, he could have had a string of girls if he'd wanted to.'

DS Fallon suddenly reappeared next to them both, her phone conversation over.

'I'm sorry, Mr Stevenson, we're going to have to leave. Something has come up. Thank you for talking to us, and we may need to catch up with you again.'

Harrison stood up; the DS had already started walking out of the room, then suddenly turned back.

'There was one final thing. Jordan Oaks received an identical invitation to yours, only his was addressed from you. I am presuming that you will tell us that you didn't send it?'

'What! No. I never sent it. No way. Seriously, I didn't send it to him.'

'Do you have any idea who might have set this whole thing up if it wasn't Jordan?'

Phil Stevenson's eyes widened as the implications of what she was saying sunk in.

'No. Why would anyone else...' His face grew paler and subconsciously he wrapped his arms around his torso.

'You're sure there was nobody thirty years ago, or now, that you can think of who might have a grudge?'

'No. We didn't hurt anyone – not purposely,' his voice was almost a whine.

'Well, thank you. If you can think of anything else that might help us with our enquiries, please get in contact straight away, and be extra vigilant, Mr Stevenson.'

With that, they left the house of Phil Stevenson, knowing full well that the DS had just put the wind up him. As they walked back to the car she explained that was exactly what she'd hoped to do. Firstly because she wondered if it might encourage him to think of anyone who would have done this, and secondly because she'd just been told that Ellie Robertson had been found dead which opened the possibility that the killer might not be finished.

TWELVE

'I don't mind snakes,' DS Fallon told Harrison as she sped, blue lights on, towards the home of Ellie Robertson. 'They're not slippery like some people think and I don't mind rats either. Wouldn't want them in my house, but I'm not going to be scared by meeting one on the street. But spiders, spiders are a whole different ball game. I don't think I could live anywhere that has bigger spiders than our British ones. It's the way they run with all those legs, or drop down from the ceiling, it totally freaks me out.'

The DS had quickly filled Harrison in on the phone call she'd received about Ellie Robertson, and then she'd put shoe leather to car accelerator and they'd set off. Harrison had found himself hanging on to the door handle in order to keep upright and not be flung either side as she wove around the traffic. DS Melinda Fallon would have given the boys on *Top Gear* a run for their money. Either that or she was a frustrated F1 driver.

Harrison tried to focus on processing their interview with Phil Stevenson. There were times when he'd clearly been holding back and had been more than economical with the truth. He definitely didn't want to talk about thirty years ago more than he had to. Having read the background notes, Harrison also knew that they'd had their group running for more than just a few months. Yet Phil had seemed genuinely shocked and surprised when the DS told him that his name had been on an invite to Jordan. Understanding why the six of them had gone back to that cave yesterday was also a critical part of the group dynamic. Phil had said that being in the group and meeting there had been exciting, clandestine, and maybe that was it, he'd gone because life as a middle-aged man with responsibilities was mundane and the temptation to relive his youth had been too strong.

As they progressed towards Ellie Robertson's flat, Harrison began to realise that the faster DS Fallon drove, the faster she talked. It was clearly some kind of concentration technique. Or at least he hoped so. He'd have been lying to himself if he didn't admit he was a little relieved when they pulled up outside the block that had once been where Ellie lived.

DS Fallon exchanged a few words with the local detective whose patch Ellie Robertson lived in. They'd been called once the seriousness of the crime had been realised, and Ellie's husband, Michael, had told him about the murder she'd witnessed the day before. The DS immediately got in touch with the incident room in case this was in any way related.

'Took a while for the reptile guys to make sure the flat was clear. We've had to evacuate the neighbours in case we didn't get them all and one's escaped through an air duct or something.' The curly-haired DS explained to them both as he led them up the stairs to the first floor. 'Just keep your eyes open when you're in there. We've got some anti-venom on standby just in case,' he added reassuringly, 'but having seen the amount of bites on the victim, we think the snakes are probably running on empty anyway.'

'What time did this all happen?'

'Not sure on exact time. The husband was out at lunch with

a relative, said Ellie hadn't felt well and wanted to stay at home. She'd been really shaken up after what happened yesterday. One of the neighbours said she saw her going out for a walk about half one so we know she was OK then. By the time her husband got home at six p.m., she was unconscious on the floor covered in snake bites. Still breathing, just, but by the time the paramedics got to her there wasn't much they could do. The venom had done too much damage.'

'They took her to the hospital?'

'Yeah. But she died on the way.'

'How did the snakes get in?'

'Well they didn't exactly knock, but they arrived in an Amazon parcel. We know that's how they came because our reptile expert was able to confirm the presence of snake poop in the box. He said they'd have been mighty angry and scared at being shoved inside the box and would have come out all fangs blazing. She didn't stand a chance. Amazing what you can buy online these days!' he added with some gallows humour.

'More than one snake then?' DS Fallon continued, ignoring the joke.

'We've bagged two. Hoping that there aren't any more, but reptile guy is still on site so if you do see anything dark and slithery, shout. He reckons they're likely to be exhausted and he just has a few more places to check, so you should be OK. Forensics are going to go in once we can definitely give them an all clear.'

With that, the detective waved them towards the flat door, but noticeably didn't follow them any further. DS Fallon and Harrison put on the obligatory forensics cover-all gear, along with some latex gloves, and stepped inside.

Some blood and vomit on the hallway floor marked the spot where Ellie Robertson had been. It had been smeared along the floor towards the door, possibly her husband had seen a snake and attempted to drag his wife to safety.

Harrison was impressed that DS Fallon was true to her

word and didn't hesitate to go into the flat, despite the best job her counterpart had done to make her nervous about there being more snakes.

They both went straight to the box first, and the DS carefully lifted some of the brown packing paper which remained inside. In the bottom, next to the offending evidence that the snakes had been trapped in there, was a broken ankh.

'Same as with Jordan,' DS Fallon said aloud. 'Do you think the killer is going after them all?' She looked up at Harrison, anxiety lighting up her eyes.

'I think that is a very real possibility that we can't risk discounting now,' he replied.

'I need to warn them,' she said immediately pulling her phone out of her pocket and dialling the incident room.

While the DS was on the phone, Harrison looked around the flat of the recently deceased Ellie Robertson. There was nothing obvious to suggest an interest in their old Set religion, or anything ancient Egyptian. No statues or paintings. Ellie, it appeared, enjoyed reading hot romance books these days rather than religious philosophy, because there was a big bookshelf full of them. On the bottom shelf, Harrison saw some photograph albums. Relics of the past nowadays with most of the photographs now digital and turned into photo books. He flicked through. One was Ellie as a child with her family on various holidays, but one book was from her uni days.

Harrison looked at the gawky, shy young woman who peered slightly to the left of the camera from underneath a thick fringe. This must have been their first few weeks at Leeds, the Freshers' Week banner behind giving him that clue. He didn't recognise anyone else, until he turned the page and saw a young Phil Stevenson and Jordan Oaks. They were sat in a bar looking like wall flowers who were too scared to even go and ask for a pint. Then, as he turned the pages, something changed. All of them seemed to bloom. Ellie had cut her hair and bleached it, and she'd started wearing make-up and clothes which showed a bit of flesh rather than being buttoned up to her chin. She stood up straight and tall, looking right down the barrel of the camera in these later photos, or in others she was staring adoringly at Jordan. There was no mistaking the newfound confidence that exuded from her.

The others were the same, seven of them all laughing at the camera which presumably Ellie held, the sun on their skin and what looked to be the hill where the cave was, in the background. This little group of theirs wasn't just a bit of fun as Phil had said, it had metamorphosed them all. Harrison could see the arrogance in their faces, this new sense of self-importance which filled them up and made them invincible. How had this invincibility been created? Was it just a few incantations and candles as Phil Stevenson had said? Was he telling the truth about Morgan Grainger's death? He died, possibly not long after the last photo in the album was taken. So was this the key? Is somebody avenging their arrogance and whatever occurred that day thirty years ago which led to Morgan losing his life?

THIRTEEN

Harrison had left DS Fallon in the incident room, co-ordinating the operation to ensure the rest of the group were safe in what was now a double murder inquiry.

He wanted to process all he had seen and heard during the day, fit together the puzzle pieces, work out what was missing and try to make sense of what appeared to be a unique group which based itself loosely on the Temple of Set, but according to Phil was not governed or sanctioned by them and had just been 'a bit of fun'.

He didn't of course take his word for it. Harrison set Ryan on the case.

A full day of being with people meant Harrison decided to have room service for his dinner. Solitude was the antidote to the overwhelm that came with too much social stimulation.

Before easing his mind though, he needed to release the tension from his body with some exercise, craving the endorphin hit that it would also bring. He'd changed immediately into his gym gear and headed to the hotel gym, which thankfully turned out to be empty except for an elderly man on one of the exercise bikes.

Harrison stretched and started with some weights, putting his big shoulders and biceps through their paces as he pumped the machine, repetition after repetition, squeezing every drop of energy from his muscles. Press-ups, planks, and squats, before more arm work with some pull-ups. By now the sweat had begun to soak into his top and his skin was coloured with the exertion.

He was aware of the old man slowly pedalling away on the static bike in the corner. His eyes watching from underneath bushy white eyebrows.

Next, Harrison wanted to push his cardiovascular system to the limit and so he got onto the treadmill, immediately turning it up to high speed. He thought of nothing else except running. Moving his legs and arms in unison, powering his body on.

When it was just becoming a struggle, he increased the incline, relishing the added burning in his lungs and legs as he challenged his body to give just a little bit more. Stride after stride. His chest heaving.

Finally, when he could feel his muscles start to become ragged, he returned the machine to flat and gradually reduced the speed, until panting, sweat dripping, he got off.

Harrison stretched his big thigh muscles while they were still warm, balancing one leg at a time to pull his leg up and back, before stretching out the calf muscles. He did similar stretches for his arms and shoulders, flexibility as important as strength.

Exercise routine over, Harrison looked up to see the old man still on the exercise bike, slowly pedalling.

'You done already?' the old man said to him. 'You youngsters have no stamina,' he said to Harrison, who wasn't sure whether he was joking or not.

'Enjoy your evening,' Harrison replied with a wave and left the man to continue his lonely cycle ride.

· · ·

When Harrison got back to his hotel room, he discovered several missed calls and messages on his mobile which he'd left by the bed.

> Attempted murder of Andy Lawson. He's OK.
> I'm heading over to speak to him.

Harrison immediately called the DS.

'We were checking on all the rest of the group but couldn't get hold of Andy Lawson and his work said he hadn't come in, which was unusual. Eventually got local uniform to go and check on him at his flat. Heard him shouting for help. He'd been stuck on top of his dining room table for five hours since receiving a similar parcel to Ellie Robertson. The killer must have dropped them off around the same time. Had an incredibly narrow escape as he spotted the snakes before he put his hands in the box. He's badly shaken up, pathological hatred of snakes apparently. Poor bloke had to stay out of harm's way for another hour while they tracked down the reptiles. He was at least able to tell us that there were two, same as we found at Ellie's, which goes some way to easing my mind that we've got them all from there.'

There was silence for a moment as Harrison took in the new information.

'Dr Lane, you there?'

'Yes. Any CCTV of the delivery driver?'

'Not so far but we're working on it. No idea how they got into either building either as they're both secured. We found another broken ankh at the bottom of the box again. He's had a very lucky escape. Anyway, while forensics work on it, I'm heading home so see you in the morning.'

Focusing on his body and exercising had given Harrison's brain the break it needed. That coupled with the endorphins which now raced around, also gave him the energy to sit back on the hotel bed and logically think through all he'd learnt in the last twenty-four hours.

The fact that the killer had struck again, but Andy didn't die, could knock them off balance. Would it make them more careless or desperate because they'd failed? For someone who had carefully planned and prepared the first two murders, it could be a turning point. Or perhaps they were more resilient than that and might just try again. Either way, it was becoming increasingly clear that the killer was working their way through the group.

When Harrison's room service Thai chicken curry arrived fifteen minutes later, he was ready to talk to Ryan.

He video called him.

'Yo, boss.' Ryan's face loomed into view on his phone. 'You eating dinner? What you having?'

Harrison took that as a positive sign. Ryan sounded hungry which meant he was probably making an effort with his diet.

'Chicken curry,' Harrison replied. He'd chosen it because it was one of the few things on the menu that didn't involve potato fries. Much as he liked them, he too was trying to eat more healthily. 'How did you get on with the Temple?'

'Yeah, fine. You were right, they haven't got one of their Pylons in that area, never have, so whatever your group were doing, it was their own show. What even is a Pylon anyway, apart from being a metal thing that holds electrical wires?'

'It's the pair of big gates to Egyptian temples and symbolises the horizon – emphasising rebirth,' Harrison replied, before taking another mouthful of curry which he was really quite enjoying.

'Right. Well, they didn't want to give me any info, not surprisingly all very secretive.'

Harrison paused before taking on board another mouthful.

'It's good that we know for sure now that they were doing

their own thing.' He couldn't resist the forkful of curry any longer.

Ryan realised he was going to need to speak.

'From the size of the candles that you sent through, we'd be looking at a minimum of twenty-four hours, possible forty-eight or more non-stop burning.'

'That ties with the evidence which suggests Jordan was strung up in that cave twenty-four hours before the rest of the group arrived. Whoever did this was well prepared.'

'I've also tracked down the Leeds University student liaison who dealt with the group after the accident. She's happy to talk.'

'That'll be useful. I saw some photos of them at the time and they really seem to have changed in just a few months from when they first started at the university, becoming confident, possibly arrogant by the end of the first year and just before the accident happened.'

'What do you think caused the accident? Were they up to something illegal?'

'Not necessarily. The whole ethos of the Temple of Set is to rise above the rest of us mere humans, and maybe they felt they were doing just that. Not sure it was reflected in their exam results though – and it may well have alienated them from the rest of the student body. As for the accident, from the official report it looked like it was just that. A minor cave in, possibly because they'd started using the cave after a long time of disuse, or it was also suggested that some particularly prolonged wet weather could have been the cause.'

'They were arrested after the incident though, weren't they?'

'Yeah, only for a bit. It was deemed accidental, but DS Fallon is trying to trace Morgan Grainger's family in case one of them has decided to exact their revenge, thirty years on.'

'Well, unfortunately, you were right about the hieroglyphs

too, just various ways of spelling Set in Egyptian. Nothing any cleverer than that, and no curses or clues as to the killer's purpose. What's your hunch?' Ryan asked, reaching for the packet of rice cakes he'd abandoned in disgust earlier, because eating them now was preferable to not eating anything while he watched Harrison tuck into a Thai curry.

'You should know I don't do hunches, Ryan, because then I risk looking for evidence to support that theory rather than finding the truth.'

Ryan smiled, having known full well that Harrison would say that, but hoped he'd come up with something anyway.

'And,' Harrison continued, 'right now, apart from the Grainger family's motive, and the obvious anniversary element, I'm not seeing a clear reason for suddenly starting this all back up again like this. Whoever it is likes symbolism and a bit of theatre. If I was Morgan's relative looking for revenge, I'd have wiped them all out when they were all together in the cave. They had opportunity. If they could build that clever booby trap to kill Jordan, then they'd have been able to prep something that could have taken out more than just one of them. Instead, they have eked it out, making the whole group watch Jordan's death. I'm getting the feeling that they want to pick them off one by one. Far more brutal and calculated than the sudden annihilation of them all.'

FOURTEEN

It was the same dream as usual. They were all in the cave's main chamber; eight red-robed figures walking around the statue of Set, invoking him to help transform their mortal bodies into the essence of divinity. Candles flickering, incense burning.

The one in the lead rang a small bell. Nine times. They walked to the centre, facing the silver pentagram, and together they summoned the elemental forces.

First, they turned to the west.

'We summon the swirling energies of water to purify this ritual.'

They turned counterclockwise to the south.

'We summon the searing flames of fire which scorch the earth.'

Another anticlockwise turn, so this time they faced the east.

'We summon the raging winds which travel the earth.'

Finally, they turned to the north.

'We summon the earth which binds our mortal bodies.'

Then the first one bent and picked up a chalice. 'Hail, Set, we invite you in.'

They drink from the chalice and pass it along the group,

each member saying the same invite and drinking, until it returned once more to the start and the leader finished its contents.

Then there is silence as each cloaked figure concentrates.

No sound except the slight hiss of their breath and the occasional drip of water in the cave. Almost pure silence at times which makes their ears throb in the effort to find something to tune into.

They stare hard at the pentagram until finally, it begins to spin and gradually they see an eye appear within it.

The leader of the group picks up the knife from the altar.

'It is time.'

One of the group has their arms taken by the two members either side and they are pushed forward towards the figure with the knife.

They hesitate, turning to the others.

'I'm not sure I want to.' But the others start chanting.

The leader walks towards them.

'No.'

But there is no turning back. No escape. The whole group crowds around them, pushing them towards the eye in the centre of the pentagram and the shining steel knife.

The blade flashes, reflecting the flickering candlelight.

One last attempt to escape, futile.

It is for the good of the group. They have been chosen. They are going to die.

FIFTEEN

Harrison had been up early and was just washing down his breakfast with the last of his orange juice. He went to the room to get organised and was back in the hotel entrance just as DS Fallon's car sped into the car park. He'd forgotten how keen she was in getting to places in record time.

As it was, the rush hour traffic kept their journey to a sensible pace, which probably wasn't a bad thing considering he'd only just eaten.

'Miracle we didn't have two bodies yesterday.' DS Fallon had greeted him as he got in.

As someone who also wasn't overly good at the social pleasantries, her lack of 'good morning' didn't faze him at all.

'The team managed to ring the rest of the group last night to warn them that they needed to be vigilant. We think we've caught all the snakes that were at Ellie Robertson's, turns out they're Egyptian cobras.'

'Those snakes aren't easy to come by,' Harrison thought aloud.

'No, but you can source them on the black web if you have the cash. I'm hoping that we'll find the trail, but I've been warned that it's going to be tough and certainly won't be quick. Andy Lawson was – unsurprisingly – incredibly relieved to have avoided Ellie's fate... Here we are.'

They had arrived outside a nice café which advertised 'the best home brew and slice in the whole of Yorkshire.' As Yorkshire prided itself on its tea, that was quite a boast.

'I've been told that Ron will be expecting a full English breakfast for his time,' DS Fallon said to Harrison as they got out and entered what turned out to be an upmarket greasy spoon with a modern twist. The full English had undergone a makeover and now included a 'light' version and a 'vegan' version, as well as a 'Mediterranean' option.

The man they'd come to see was sitting reading a newspaper in one of the red leather booth seats. He folded the paper up as they approached and then stood to shake their hands.

They introduced themselves and both sat down opposite the retired detective who immediately looked to Harrison.

'So you SIO?' he asked him.

'No. DS Fallon is SIO. I'm here in an advisory capacity from the Ritualistic Behavioural Crime unit with the NCA.'

'Bloody hell, whatever next. Never had that in my time. There's always an ism or a label for every type of behaviour these days, as if we never had a range of folks in times gone,' the former DI said to him, before turning to DS Fallon. 'You're a bit young to be tackling a murder inquiry, aren't you, love?'

'Age can be deceptive.' She smiled back at him, not rising to the jibe.

Ron Norman was in his seventies, had a nice healthy suntan which was just one indicator that he was retired. The other was a round paunch, which showed he'd stopped running around chasing criminals and instead taken to sitting around.

Just then the waitress came over to take their order. DS Fallon asked for a coffee, while Harrison had a mint tea. Ron went for the light full English.

'Doctor's orders,' he said to them both, patting his stomach. 'Too much visceral fat he tells me. Put on the pounds after retiring. I need to lower my cholesterol and do more exercise. Anyways, so you want to talk to me about the *Students of Satan*, do you?'

'I've never heard them referred to as that, except in the media,' DS Fallon replied.

'It was our name for 'em. Used to worship the dark Lord, as they called him, with pentagrams and sacrifices and the like.'

'Your name, as in the investigating team?'

'Yup. Media stole it from us,' he added looking pleased about the fact.

'Did they ever mention Satan by name?' Harrison asked now.

'Not in as many words. Said it was some Egyptian god that was around thousands of years before Christianity, and he was the true dark Lord. Made my skin creep.'

'You said sacrifices, what sacrifices were they doing?'

'Not sure. Rabbits, I think. There was blood daubed on the walls of the cave, pictures like you'd get in an Egyptian tomb.'

'Did it look like this?' DS Fallon pulled out her phone and showed him some images from their recent crime scene.

'Yeah, that's it. That's exactly it. Is that from the other day?'

She nodded as he shook his head and frowned.

'We had the whole lot cleared out after the accident. With the media coverage, there was suddenly coach-loads of people walking in the area and wanting to visit the satanic caves. Local tourist agency loved it and the authorities were forced to clear the rockfall and make the place safe. We had all the satanic stuff taken away.'

'Was there any suspicion that the rockfall was anything but accidental?'

'Oh yeah plenty. But we couldn't find any evidence to prove it. The lad's family were all over it, threatening to sue, calling for the other students to be put on trial. It all got a bit fraught.'

'You're referring to Morgan Grainger's family?'

Ron Norman nodded.

The conversation paused for a few moments as the waitress brought their drinks and then his breakfast.

'Did Morgan have any siblings?' Harrison asked.

'No. Only child. They totally doted on him.'

'But no charges were ever brought?' DS Fallon continued, knowing full well what the answer was but wanting to hear it from Ron.

'No. We couldn't make anything stick. Verdict was it was just kids messing about, that's all. We couldn't find anything illegal and the geologists said the rockfall was just a natural occurrence so the investigation was dropped. But what they were doing wasn't moral, I can tell you that. And leopards don't change their spots. Doesn't surprise me one iota,' he said, shaking a grilled tomato at her on the end of his fork, 'that they're back and doing it all again.'

'Why were they arrested then if you had nothing to say they were involved?'

Ron put his fork and knife down for a moment and leaned in a little closer. 'We think that there were a few hours between the rockfall happening and us getting there. That the rest of the group left the caves and only went back and called it in a few hours later.'

'Why would they do that?'

Ron raised his eyebrows at her. 'Getting rid of incriminating evidence, that's why. Their red cloaks were found in a bin not far from their halls.'

'But they left the cave as it was, the statue and things; wouldn't they have got rid of all that if they'd wanted to hide it all?'

Ron shrugged his shoulders. 'Initially they tried to tell us that it was just a play they were practising, wanted to do some am dram. We soon saw through that of course. I'm telling you, they weren't the innocents they said they were.'

'Well, he's a dinosaur,' DS Fallon muttered the second they were out of earshot. Having settled the bill, they'd left Ron Norman to finish his breakfast and newspaper alone.

'And now we know why the media called them satanic and wrote lurid headlines,' Harrison added, grateful that he was working in this day and age when there was a little more understanding of alternative religions – even if it wasn't completely there yet.

'Also explains why there's very little in the archive about it. The case must have been dropped quite early on. From all the media coverage, I'd have expected a bit more. I know we shouldn't make assumptions or point the finger, but I'd like to bet that Ron and his gang were a bit annoyed when the case had to be dropped and fed all that Students of Satan stuff to the media.'

'I think you're absolutely right, and perhaps the parents of Morgan Grainger were also stoking that particular fire, aided by Ron.'

DS Fallon sighed.

'Yeah, although unfortunately we can't ask them as they're both dead now. I'm hoping that the Student Liaison Officer you've told us about will throw some light on what went on. We're due to see her this afternoon, although first I've asked to speak with Dermot O'Connelly and Paige Nicholson. We'll give Andy Lawson a break for today after his ordeal yesterday.'

DS Fallon was about to continue talking, but her phone rang. She picked it up on her in-car system.

'Detective Sergeant, I need to see you immediately. Have you seen today's news?' There was no mistaking the less-than-amused tone of Detective Superintendent Julian Smith.

Harrison looked out the side window as DS Fallon's cheeks flushed.

'No, sir, I haven't. I've been interviewing. I'm just on my way in now.'

'Well I'd suggest you hurry it up.'

The call ended and for once there was silence in the car.

'Is he always like that?' Harrison asked gently.

'Yeah, with me he is,' DS Fallon answered. 'It's fine, I'm used to it.'

But Harrison didn't think she was – and more importantly, she shouldn't have to be.

DS Fallon disappeared into Smith's office and Harrison caught up with all the evidence that had been gathered late yesterday and early this morning, including the new material from the attack on Andy Lawson. Witness statements and CCTV were distinctly lacking, which was frustrating. The team were still trying to track down cameras around the vicinity of Ellie and Andy's flats in an attempt to catch the delivery driver, but up to now it was proving difficult.

The snakes were confirmed as being Egyptian cobras, one of the most venomous in the world. By putting two in each box, Harrison guessed the killer was making sure help couldn't reach the victims in time. It had certainly worked with Ellie, and Andy Lawson must be counting his lucky stars this morning that he wasn't on Betty's metal gurney at the morgue as well.

Question was, would the killer try to hit Andy again or move on to another victim – assuming that was their plan. DS Fallon had put in extra security measures and warned all of the members of the group that their lives could be in danger. Forewarned was definitely forearmed, but without any idea as to the killer's agenda and motive, there was no way of knowing if they did have another target and if so, when they might strike.

Detective Superintendent Julian Smith strode through the office, DS Fallon trailing in his wake.

'He's called a press conference,' she said to Harrison as she passed. 'You might want to come along in case you spot anything. It's outside in half an hour.' Then she sat down next to him and whispered, 'I have no idea how the press got hold of this story. I honestly don't believe that anyone in my team would have leaked the details, but they've got a couple of bits of inside information which means it must have come from this building.'

'None of the group could have spoken out?'

She shook her head. 'No, there were a couple of details that they wouldn't have known. One was the makeup of the booby trap in the cave, which could have only come from the forensic report, and the other was a line about Jordan having been 'taken' to the cave which made me suspicious. It's only us who know his car was still at his house, everyone else assumed he'd driven there like them. A reporter wouldn't have had the time to dig up this info on their own and it's all been nicely linked to what happened thirty years ago. Smith is furious and blames me for running a loose team. Said he's going to have to keep a closer eye on the investigation going forwards.'

She looked both childlike and older than her years in that moment. Her body deflated and folded in on itself in the chair. She was staring at her hands in her lap, her thumb stroking the band of her engagement ring.

'Anyway, I'm just going to have a chat with the team, let

them know what's going on.' DS Fallon stood up, the mask replaced.

Harrison watched her leave and a little later wandered outside to the front of the police station where the media were gathering for the press conference. He stood across the other side of the narrow road where he could watch everyone. The initial newspaper story had alerted all the rest of the media to the news and so they'd turned out in force. A Sky News mobile broadcast van was parked next to one from the BBC and the Detective Superintendent eventually came to stand in front of the sea of cameras and microphones.

Harrison watched him, but he also kept a close eye on the crowd. Killers were known to go along to events like this, where they could bask in the incognito glory of their work.

The statement from Smith was standard official speak, he looked directly at all the cameras and journalists, clearly enjoying the limelight. Certainly not looking like he was hating every second of the publicity as he'd told DS Fallon. It was at the end during questions that Harrison got annoyed.

'So, is this a revival of the Students of Satan?' one of the reporters asked.

Instead of immediately ruling this out and chastising the reporter over their terminology, Smith encouraged it. 'We are certainly seeing some links to the past and I would urge anyone to come forward with information about the events of thirty years ago and anything unusual that they might have perhaps felt too frightened to talk about then. The retired Detective Inspector who led that case was convinced that there had been more to what happened than we were able to prove, but our forensic techniques have substantially improved since then and I will get to the truth. There is no place for satanic cults in Yorkshire.'

Harrison looked at DS Fallon's face, which even from across

the road he could see was taught with anger. He took his phone out and typed a message to Ryan.

SIXTEEN

Dermot O'Connelly agreed to meet Harrison and DS Fallon in a small coffee shop on the outskirts of Leeds, because he said he was currently staying at an undisclosed location given the threat to his life. Their journey there had been spent mostly in silence, the DS clearly struggling with the interference of her boss and trying to think through the situation with the media.

Dermot had stationed himself in the darkest corner of the coffee shop and had already worked his way through a large cappuccino before they'd arrived. DS Fallon bought a new round, this time with Dermot's new preference of a large hot chocolate.

'I saw what happened to Jordan and heard about Ellie and Andy. There's no way I'm going anywhere near my flat until you've caught whoever did this. I'm going off-grid,' he said to them both as though he was quoting a line from an action spy movie.

'I understand your concern, Mr O'Connelly, but please do stay in contact with us. We need to know you're safe and you need to be able to call for help if you need it.'

He'd nodded, sniffed and scanned the room as though the killer could be watching them right there and then.

'Do you have any idea who might be doing this? Someone from thirty years ago perhaps?' the DS continued.

'Oh great, so that means you lot don't have a scooby yet in terms of a suspect. That bodes well! I thought you were the detectives.'

'I'm asking because we need to find a motive and we believe that it relates to what happened thirty years ago, which the group has been a little cagey about.'

Harrison was impressed with DS Fallon's patience.

Dermot shrugged, refusing to be drawn, and shook his head. 'No idea. Just wish I'd never answered that invite and gone to that bloody cave again.'

'That seems to be a sentiment the others share. So why did you all go? I find it hard to understand why after thirty years of not seeing each other after a shocking accident, which must have had a big impact on you all, that you suddenly decide it's a great time for a reunion at the very place where it all happened?'

'Yeah, I can see why you'd think that.' He looked down a little wistfully. 'There was something once, you know.' He lifted his head and focused on them both. 'We were young, away from home for the first time, enjoying our newfound freedom and growing up. We were pretty inseparable for a while.'

'Inseparable and invincible?' Harrison queried.

'What do you mean?' Dermot asked, turning to focus just on the big man in front of him.

'I mean, did you all think you were invincible, did you buy into the whole Set philosophy that you were all above everyone else and could achieve anything?'

Dermot thought for a moment, 'Maybe, I guess. Can't say it was my finest hour. Some undergrads drank themselves stupid in the bars, we tried to find enlightenment. It wasn't so awful, was it?'

When neither of them answered him, he continued as though trying to excuse himself.

'I studied law, you know. Not because I wanted to but because it was expected of me. Well, I'm an artist now and I don't subscribe to all the materialistic things others crave. In the long run it hasn't done me any harm – until now.'

'Were there any romantic relationships in the group?' Harrison continued.

'Nothing that actually got physical. It was all pretty pathetic really. Andy was in love with Paige, but she and Ellie were both infatuated with Jordan and nobody else ever got a look-in. Jordan, well, I think he was in love with Morgan, but he'd never have admitted to anything like that. I had my theories about him.'

'What about Phil and Kelly?'

'Phil didn't seem to have a big preference, I think he'd have grabbed any girl who showed him interest, but it certainly wouldn't have been Kelly. She was always impenetrable. Made of steel that woman is.'

'And yourself?'

'Me? A bit of a crush on Paige; she was a nice girl and pretty, hard not to like her. But I'd had a long-term relationship at home with a girl. Broke it off after I left for uni and I wasn't in a rush to get back into another one.'

Harrison wondered if that was a bit of bluff. Would Paige have even considered him as a partner anyway?

'Jordan was the leader of the group?' DS Fallon continued.

'Yeah, he started it all, a mate of his gave him the information, one night we all went down the pub and Jordan told us about it; it sounded exciting. We all agreed to join in that evening. It was a pretty momentous night. I think up to that point we'd all been struggling a bit but that evening in the pub we just gelled and the group was born. But Kelly was the one who probably took it the most seriously. She was driven.'

'In what way was she driven?'

'Ah you know, she insisted we did everything absolutely right, dressed right, said the right words and in the right order. All that sort of thing.'

'And what happened that day thirty years ago in the cave?' DS Fallon asked now.

'We were doing a ritual, nothing dodgy, and the ceiling in the tunnel started falling. We rushed to get out and it came down on us. Morgan and Andy took the brunt of it. We all got bruises and stuff, but Morgan... Well, you know.'

'What was the ritual?' Harrison asked him.

'Now you're asking. It was thirty years ago and I've put all that behind me! Something to do with passing exams I think.' Dermot shuffled in his chair. 'It was a load of shite anyway. Don't see my life full of riches and me existing on some higher cerebral level, do you? A few of them seem to have done alright but the magic certainly didn't work for me, and it sure didn't for Morgan.'

'Morgan's death must have hit you hard?'

'Yeah. He was just eighteen. Whole life ahead of him. You just don't think about dying when you're that age, not until it's shoved right in your face like that.'

Harrison let his words hang between them a moment, despite thirty years passing they were still full of emotion and regret.

'Did it make you change your view on life?' he asked him eventually.

'Certainly made me drop all that Temple of Set stuff. I'm a Buddhist now,' Dermot replied, as though challenging him. 'I use it in my art quite a lot.'

'What kind of art do you do, Mr O'Connelly?' DS Fallon sounded interested.

'Street art. Actually if you look out the window, you'll see one of my pieces just across the road there.'

All three of them looked out the window. DS Fallon and Harrison weren't sure what they were looking for, but the only thing they could see was a large graffiti painting that took up a fairly big chunk of the opposing wall. It featured a giant multi-coloured bear sitting on a small man. Harrison wasn't quite sure of the message; he knew there must be one but he couldn't see any Buddhist references.

'My tag is Karma; you might have seen some of my other work. Got a lovely heaven spot just by the swimming pool on the old warehouse. You'd have passed it on the way here.'

'Heaven spot?' DS Fallon queried.

'Up high, council won't bother to remove it which means they're sweet spots to use, but they're not easy spots to work on. If you fall, you're going to heaven,' Dermot smirked. 'Course I don't suppose I should be telling you any of this, but I figure you're too busy with catching murderers to try to stop some citizen artistry.'

'I know the spot you mean – how did you get up there to do that? I've often wondered.'

Dermot winked at her. 'Well, helps if you're a climbing champion, doesn't it? I can get up and down buildings safely in seconds. Climbed some of the toughest rock faces in the world over the years. That warehouse was like a walk in the park for me. Gives me a bit of an advantage over some of the others.'

'Do you make a living with this?' the DS asked, genuinely interested.

'If you make a name for yourself, yeah of course. You'll be commissioned for pieces and you can sell original works – you all know Banksy.'

'Yes, of course,' she said. 'Hmmm, interesting, thank you.'

'Have you given up law totally?' Harrison asked, keen to understand Dermot a little more.

'Yeah, did it for about ten years after uni, nearly drained my soul sitting in an office arguing for one word change in a sentence. My father died and I guess that freed me. He'd worked all his life in law, long hours when we didn't see him at home. Died six months after he retired. All the plans my parents had to travel and spend time together – gone. Didn't want to end up like that so I quit and went travelling for a bit.'

Dermot's face betrayed the impact the death of his father still had on him.

'What did your father think about the group?' Harrison tested.

Dermot stared at him defiantly. 'What do you think? Disappointed in me. Ashamed. That's why I cut all ties to the others.'

'How did you feel?'

'What, about the group?'

Harrison nodded and Dermot looked away into the distance before turning back and shrugging.

'Like I said, we were young and probably a bit foolish. That's all there is to know.'

'I think someone is fond of the ganja, don't you?' DS Fallon raised her eyebrows to Harrison as they left the café and Dermot behind.

'Yes, I smelt it. It's a part of his lifestyle, fits the anti-establishment attitude.'

'Yeah I guess, He's a bit of a caricature in some ways and totally different to Phil Stevenson or Andy Lawson. I never got to talk to Jordan Oaks, but I wouldn't have put them as friends either.'

'Lots of people are a bit more bohemian in their youth and then get more conformist as they get older and need to get a job and a mortgage. From the photos in Ellie's album, Dermot looks like he's done the opposite. Started off studying law and heading into corporate territory and then took a left turn.'

'He wasn't overly complimentary about our next interviewee. Made of steel he said. I wonder what she's going to say about him.'

SEVENTEEN

'The man has no backbone. Never has.' Kelly Watts left no punches in her verdict of Dermot O'Connelly.

They had gone to meet Ms Watts at her office. Neither DS Fallon or Harrison had ever been into a place of work where the boss's sealed-off office area had privacy glass in it, meaning she could look out and watch the rest of her workers, but they couldn't see in. The entire place was immaculate. Desks clear, no personal items cluttering desks or screens. There was a muted air of military precision, no young people among the staff, and they'd clearly not subscribed to the post-Covid trend of relaxed dressing. Most of the men were suited with ties, and there wasn't a pair of trainers amongst them – male or female.

'I can't be long. I work from home in the afternoons,' had been the first thing she said to them as they walked in. Harrison had a vision of the office erupting into party mode the second she walked out the door.

She was a tall, straight woman, and Harrison couldn't help being reminded of a steel pole. There were no curves to her, no soft edges. Even her hair looked like it could be made of steel wool. It was stiff and curled, a mixture of black and silver grey.

Woe betide a hair that moved out of place – it would probably have been plucked out by the root.

'Thank you for your time, Ms Watts, but this is now a double murder inquiry,' DS Fallon pointed out, 'and as I understand my colleagues have communicated to you, we believe the killer might not yet have finished.'

Kelly sat down and shut up then, although even her silence sounded like a challenging reproach.

'Have you seen any of the other members of the group in the last thirty years?'

'No. First time I'd set eyes on any of them, apart from occasionally bumping into them at uni during my second and third years, was the day before yesterday.'

'Then can I ask why you went to meet up with Jordan Oaks and the others? Why bother if you no longer had a friendship with any of them?'

Kelly hmphed. 'Well, yes, I've asked myself that question, but I guess it boiled down to plain simple inquisitiveness. He said on the invite that there was something we should see.'

'What did you think that might be?'

'I didn't know. Hence why I decided to go.'

'Was it something you were worried about, something that could have come out about what happened thirty years ago?'

DS Fallon was really trying now. Harrison could see that Kelly wound her up. She didn't show it in the sense that anyone else would notice, but he did. There was an extra edge to her questioning.

'What do you mean come out? What happened thirty years ago is done and dusted.'

'My colleagues thought that there was more of a case to answer back then,' Fallon continued to prod.

'Well in that case, why didn't they do something about it? I'll tell you why, it's because it was just an accident and we did nothing wrong.' Kelly's jaw was firmly set.

'So who would be wanting to kill members of the group now, thirty years on?'

'I don't know. I really don't know. Believe me, if I did, then I would tell you. I don't fancy death by snake bite.'

'How did you all meet at uni?' Harrison asked even though they'd already been given the answer by the others. He wanted to understand the group dynamics and whether they all had the same opinions of each other.

'We were in the same halls of residence. You don't get to choose where you're staying when you first start and I have to say they weren't my normal crowd, but one night we all went to the pub down the road and we found common ground.'

'Common ground? You mean the Temple of Set philosophy?'

'Yes, but we did our own thing. Took the principles of the church and made them our own.'

'Can you tell me how you deviated?'

Kelly looked away. 'To be honest, I can't remember and it's not the sort of thing I'd discuss.'

'Why not, are you still practising the principles of the Set religion?'

'That depends on what you mean by practising. I have followed a strict mental and physical regime that has helped me to become the successful person that I am today.'

'So you think people like us are inferior?' Harrison asked her.

DS Fallon looked at him, shocked at the question, but Kelly seemed unfazed.

'I don't think you care what I think about you. If you're asking me, do I believe myself to be a higher being than most other humans, then yes. I work hard to instil the discipline needed to attain a higher self.'

'Do you think the rest of us are heading for self-destruction then?'

'Turn on the news, Dr Lane. There is your answer. Wars, floods, famines, droughts. One group of humans destroying another group. Humanity is on the edge. It's returning to an animal-like state where we don't respect each other. One side thinks nothing of killing the other side's children and glorying in the death of its enemies. Only by attaining a higher consciousness will we survive – the human race itself is doomed and it's taking the world down with it.'

'I'm not a follower of any religion, but I have to say you've got a point there,' Harrison replied. 'But, if you were focused on self-betterment, didn't that make for a fractured group? Increase competitiveness?'

'No. You don't understand what it means to become a higher being.'

'I suspect it means leaving those who are not deserving behind. Did all the other group members disappoint you?'

Kelly shrugged and looked him in the eye. 'As you know, we've all gone our separate ways. I took my path and I'm happy with my own company.'

'I thought you were all friends.' It was DS Fallon's turn to goad her.

'We were but some of us have moved on and grown up. Dermot reaffirmed my opinion of him the other day. Thirty years hasn't improved him, it's made him soft and needy.'

'Was he always like that?' Harrison quizzed.

'Pretty much, yes. Just now he's rejected any kind of discipline and authority. He at least had some purpose in those days.'

'And the rest of the group?'

'Phil's pretty much what I expected. He's still trying to be something he's not, the big man with money and respect. Andy went off the rails for a while, but he seems to have regained his discipline. Paige is just Paige. She's an open book. Ellie and Jordan, well...'

'You know if there is something that you're not telling us about what happened thirty years ago, then I would seriously reconsider because it could be the killer's motive and if we don't know...'

'I've told you, DS Fallon. Nothing happened. There is nothing to tell apart from the fact there was an accident. Nothing illegal went on. We didn't sacrifice anybody.'

'She's a cheerful one. Remind me to never invite her round for dinner!' DS Fallon sarcastically muttered as they left.

'It's not hard to see how she would have challenged Jordan for the leadership of their group. But they all still get very defensive when we ask any details about the rituals. None of them will discuss them.'

'Yes, and the more I think about it, the more I believe that there was something that didn't come out, something they wanted hidden, and something they were afraid that Jordan was going to reveal. Most of them didn't give a toss about each other, hadn't probably thought about the others for thirty years and yet they turn up to a remote cave which must hold some pretty bad memories.'

'Agreed. There had to be something compelling to get them there.'

'You can also see why Ron Norman took against them and called them the Students of Satan. I find Ms Watts scary in broad daylight, let alone dressed up in a red cloak in a dark candlelit cave. None of this is getting us any closer to finding out who the killer might be and what the motive is, but perhaps it has to do with their secret.' DS Fallon sighed.

'Any news on Morgan's relatives?'

'Not yet. I've also got the team trying to see if we can find out who the mystery man was that gave Jordan that information thirty years ago. Who's to say that he's not suddenly decided that what they did with it was out of order and so now he has to punish them. I'm hoping we can get to see Jordan's mother to ask if she knows. But in the meantime, we're going to go and visit Janet Sutherland, the Leeds student liaison your assistant tracked down. I just hope she can give us some straight answers.'

EIGHTEEN

Ryan loved it when he could be a little bit creative with his work, and the task that Harrison had set him allowed him to be just that. Working in law enforcement meant that he had to stick by the rules. Evidence gathered illegally was not going to be admissible in a court case, even if he was tempted to cut corners at times. However, this was something different and an opportunity for him to be as clever and devious as he wanted to be.

For this work, he used his own laptop and not the NCA computers. He was good at covering his trail but there was no telling when someone might be watching what he was doing online at work. Once he was done, he called Harrison.

'Yo, boss, it's all set up,' he said to him.

'Good. I'll set things in motion my end. Thanks, Ryan,' Harrison replied, and that had been it.

Ryan leaned back in his chair, stretched, and looked at the time. It was lunch, although he hadn't really needed to look at the clock to know that because his stomach was already shouting about the fact. For a moment his fingers hovered over ordering something proper tasty, getting a delivery of noodles or a pizza, but the fantasy was disturbed by a knock on his door.

After last year's run-in with the gang, Ryan was on high alert. He said nothing but quietly crossed to his front door and peered through the peephole to see who was outside.

Standing there was his neighbour, Lisa, with a bag over her shoulder and a small furry bundle. She knocked again.

'Who is it?' Ryan called out, knowing full well who it was but wondering why she was knocking on his door. They'd said hello to each other a few times as they'd crossed paths en route to picking up post or putting the rubbish out. She seemed OK, definitely no sign of drug use and no dodgy visitors going to her flat. She'd told him she was an actress, but as she seemed to be home most days and evenings, he didn't think she was getting much work.

'Hi, Ryan, it's Lisa from number three,' she said to the door. 'Need your help with something. Please.'

Ryan hesitated, what if there was somebody else there, just out of view, who was waiting to force entry as soon as he opened the door to Lisa?

'Ryan?' she called again.

Ryan tried to think like Harrison, looking at her face and body language. Was she under duress? Was she agitated? It wasn't easy trying to ascertain anything through the tiny peephole. He picked up the taser stick he'd acquired from the private security guys who'd helped him out last time. It wasn't legal but that didn't bother him. If anyone tried to force entry to his flat then that wasn't legal either.

Then, he unbolted the door, but left the chain on – it wouldn't hold if someone really wanted to get in, but it would give him enough time to act.

'Hi, Ryan.' Lisa peered through the gap in the door at him. 'I'm sorry but I'm desperate. I have to go away for a few days and someone gave me this kitten. I can't take her and I can't leave her. Please, would you just look after her for me? She's no trouble.'

Lisa looked pleadingly at him and thrust a tiny little scrap of a kitten at the six-inch gap in the door. The kitten was so teeny that it nearly fitted through and Ryan was worried that Lisa might try shoving her in. He unchained the door and hoped that this wasn't a ruse.

'Thanks so much,' Lisa said, interpreting the door opening as his agreement. All of a sudden, he was face to face with a little wide-eyed tabby kitten, which looked at him and mewed.

'I don't know what to do,' he blurted, but Lisa had propelled the cat towards his arms and so he found himself taking hold of it rather than letting it fall.

'Honestly, it's easy, you can look up instructions online. I've got some food for her in this bag.'

'Can't someone else...' Ryan tried to push back, but Lisa was already backing away.

'Thanks so much, Ryan, I really owe you. It's just for a couple of days and I'll be back.'

As Ryan was still standing there, not looking as though he was happy about the situation, Lisa put the bag on the floor by his feet.

'She's adorable, you'll love her. I've got to go,' Lisa added, and with that she turned and went straight back into her flat before he could say another word.

Ryan stood there a few more seconds, contemplating walking across the landing and knocking on Lisa's door to say he couldn't do this, but something about the little warm fur ball in his arms made him stop. It was only for a couple of days after all, and a kitten couldn't hurt him. He'd manage. He picked up the bag, which was surprisingly heavy, cats must need a lot of stuff, closed the door and re-bolted all the locks.

For a few moments he stood holding the little kitten out in

front of him. He had no idea how old she was but she was tiny with four white paws and a white tip on her tail. What was he supposed to do with her though? Did she have fleas? He really didn't want to have fleas in the flat. Where was she going to go to the toilet? He didn't have a garden on the first floor. Were they even allowed to have pets? He'd have to check his lease. What was her name?

Ryan was still standing there when he heard Lisa's door bang again and so he peered through the peephole, wondering if she'd changed her mind and was about to take away this responsibility he'd found himself holding. She didn't even glance at his door. He was just in time to see her struggling down the stairs with two big heavy suitcases. That was a lot of luggage for just a few days!

With one arm he picked up the bag Lisa had given him, the kitten nestled into the crook of the other. Lunch was forgotten. Ryan unpacked the bag which contained a litter tray, cat litter, food and some paperwork which showed the kitten had received some injections. Strange that Lisa had felt it necessary to give him that if she was only away for a few days. Maybe she didn't fully trust him to look after the cat properly and so might need to take it to the vets.

There was no bed in the bag so Ryan created a little nest out of cushions on the sofa and placed the kitten on that. It seemed reluctant to be put down, but eventually curled up and fell straight asleep. He stood looking at it for a few moments. He'd never had a pet of his own, never looked after anything in his life, not even a goldfish. Now here was a little living thing that was reliant on him.

Ryan got online immediately and typed *How to look after a kitten*, into Google.

NINETEEN

Janet Sutherland lived in a bungalow in a relatively quiet suburb of Leeds. She opened the door wearing an apron that read, *Saving one life at a time.*

'I'm so sorry, I was running late. It was my morning shift at the charity shop and they were short staffed. Come in. Come in. I'll just be a moment while I take this off. Do you want a tea?' Janet waved them into a sitting room area as she disappeared up the hallway.

'Cuppa would be lovely, thanks,' Melinda replied. Driving around and interviewing everyone had dried out her throat and Kelly Watts had certainly not been inclined to offer them a drink. She couldn't get rid of them fast enough. While they'd grabbed a drink at lunch, they were still behind on the hydration levels.

'Just a water please,' Harrison added for himself.

The pair of them walked into a sitting room that spoke of a family life well lived. Children in dated photographs led on to grandchildren in bright new ones, with a group shot of six adults and Janet, plus two babies and two toddlers. A photograph – that Harrison estimated was about ten or fifteen years old – of Janet and a man exchanging a lovely hug, also took centre stage. Other than that photograph, there was no sign of a man living in the house. Just one chair was sunken in and worn on the arms. A basket of knitting on one side and a side table with the TV remote and a cold cup of tea on the other. This wasn't a divorce, it was bereavement.

The pair of them sat down on the sofa, which was the only other major piece of furniture in the room.

'Here we go.' Janet soon bustled in. 'Tea for you, detective, and a glass of water. I've brought some biscuits too. I'm a bit peckish after my shift. Help yourselves.'

Harrison and DS Fallon looked at the plate of biscuits and both thought that they shouldn't. Both also reached out and took one, the temptation too much.

'Thanks so much for agreeing to see us, Mrs Sutherland,' DS Fallon started after a quick swig of the brown Yorkshire tea.

'That's quite alright, love. I'm not sure I'm going to be much help to you, I've been retired seven years and the accident was thirty years ago now. And please, call me Janet.'

Janet Sutherland had a kind face, a woman in her seventies with soft wrinkled skin that showed plenty of creases around her eyes and mouth from a lifetime of smiles lighting up her face.

'We wanted some insight really into what the group was like. What kind of people were they and whether there was anyone else who might have born a grudge against them.'

'Grudge? Well that's an interesting one. So, what were they like? They were an odd crew. On face value they had nothing in common, but they found some kind of bond between them. Didn't take much to break that, mind,' Janet began. 'Welfare wasn't as advanced in those days as it is now, especially mental health support, but we tried to keep an eye out for any potential issues with new students in particular, and during exam times.' She took a bite of her biscuit and thought for a few moments.

'Did you have any alarm bells about any of the eight group members?'

Janet shook her head and swallowed. 'Nope. No complaints from other students, and no known issues with them. It was only after the accident that everything blew up.'

'The police investigation was dropped though, it was just treated as an accident, so why was so much fuss made?'

'Ah well, there's a few good reasons for that.' Janet settled back in her chair. 'Firstly, if you ask me, I don't think they called the emergency services straight away. Now I'm not saying that it was as easy as it is now. Students couldn't afford mobile phones in those days, they weren't as common and cheap as they are now; although I believe Morgan had one as his parents were a little better off than the other families. But anyways, when I first spoke to Paige, she blurted out that they'd gone back to the halls and then returned to the cave before calling for help. There were countless phone boxes in between that cave and the halls. Now she immediately denied she'd said that to me and none of the others backed up that story, but I know what she said.'

'Why do you think that would be?'

'Because they wanted to get rid of some evidence from their rooms.'

'But you have no way of confirming that?'

Janet shook her head. 'No. Nothing was ever found but when you went into their rooms it was clear that things were missing, do you know what I mean? Gaps where things once were and the like. Those rooms are only small and they tend to be crammed full of stuff. I don't think most people would notice but I'd been in hundreds of those student flats, had kids of my own too, and I'm telling you that something was not quite right.'

'You said there were a few reasons?'

'Yes. The second reason is the nature of what they were up to in that cave. The national newspapers got hold of the story and photographers somehow got in. It was certainly not what I would want my children doing, and so they were besieged by reporters and paparazzi. They all went into hiding and must have had their ears bent by their families. Morgan's parents went totally nuclear, I think the youngsters call it nowadays. They threatened to sue the university for allowing their son to be pulled into a cult. Used the media to stir things up. Things got very ugly.'

'That's interesting, and it was just Morgan's parents who were angry?'

'All the parents got involved to varying degrees, some more bothered than others, but it was Mr and Mrs Grainger who made the most noise. They were older, I think Morgan had come along later in their lives and he was their only son. He was their world. I have to say that out of all of them, Morgan was the most mainstream, I suppose you could say. But I think he was more impressionable, probably because his parents had molly-coddled him and kept him a little too sheltered from the world.'

'You say Morgan was an only child, did you ever meet any other relatives or friends?'

Janet thought and shook her head.

'Where were the family from?'

'Windsor area I believe. Berkshire.'

'And what about the others? If Morgan was the most main-stream, what kind of personalities were they?'

'Oh nothing too odd, if you know what I mean, but a couple of them were quite withdrawn and shy. I didn't take to that Kelly; she was like an ice maiden. Jordan was clearly the one they all looked up to and I'd say a little arrogant, that kind of arrogance of the young who suddenly find themselves out in the world without boundaries – although Phillip Stevenson could give him a run for his money. He was ambitious. Andy and Dermot were fine. I suppose Dermot was a little downbeat, more of a glass half empty kind of chap. And of course Andy was injured as well. But there was an edge to them all after the accident. Maybe they were scared of getting into trouble because they were arrested initially, or maybe it was something else. And it wasn't just them, we were all under siege for a bit with the media attention, and then when the police investigation was dropped, they just crawled back to their holes and things calmed down. Once we'd dealt with Morgan's parents of course. He never finished his degree, but the others did.'

'There was obviously a good reason why Morgan couldn't finish his degree, but did the others stay at Leeds and stick together as a group?'

'No they all split up, none of them shared a house or halls in the second year. They stayed on and got their degrees though. But there was no reason why Morgan couldn't have finished his degree, the university were going to give him special dispensation because of the accident; it's just his parents didn't want him anywhere near the others. I dare say that had he been able to make the decision, he'd have stayed on.'

'What do you mean? Morgan was killed.' DS Fallon leant forward in her chair.

'Oh no, that was just the story that was told publicly. He was in a coma for a couple of days, looked like he was dead, but when the police case was dropped, of course everyone and the interest disappeared. The parents threatened the Dean. Said he either spread it about that Morgan never survived his injuries, or they'd take the university to court. As the police case was over, he just let that be the narrative. They didn't want any of the others trying to contact Morgan, you see. They wanted a clean break for him and the easiest way to ensure that was for the rest of the group to think he was dead.'

DS Fallon and Harrison looked at each other in amazement.

'Are you sure?' DS Fallon asked Janet.

'Yes, absolutely sure, love. He was in hospital a fair while, much longer than Andy was, and so it was easy just to hide him from the others. His parents had him moved anyway to a hospital near Windsor. I thought you'd have known that.' She looked from one to the other. 'But then I guess people just accepted it and nobody thought to check as there was no police investigation going on. Not morally right in my view. The others have spent the last thirty years thinking their friend died. That must hang on at least some of their consciences, but the Graingers were very insistent.'

The expletives that left DS Fallon's mouth after they'd thanked Mrs Sutherland and left, said it all.

'Why did we not know that?' she said to Harrison, not blaming him but airing her frustration. She got on the phone immediately and alerted the team to track down Morgan Grainger, who had just become their number one suspect.

TWENTY

DS Fallon and her team went into overdrive with the revelation that Morgan Grainger had survived the cave rockfall. It didn't take a genius to come up with the idea that he could be exacting revenge for what had happened to him thirty years ago. The question was, where was he and what had he been doing for the past thirty years?

Tracking him down via his parents was a no-go – they had both died and the family home been sold. The investigating team were trying to speak to the solicitor who'd sorted out the probate and will, to see if they had a forwarding address for their son, Morgan.

Detective Superintendent Julian Smith was on the war path and he wanted DS Fallon's scalp.

'Fallon. In my office,' he shouted.

'We're supposed to be talking to Paige Nicholson in an hour, can you go along without me and see what you can find out?' she'd quickly said to Harrison. 'It's Andy Lawson later this afternoon, hopefully I can join you for that.'

Then she'd quickly scurried across the incident room and

everyone there heard Smith admonishing her before he closed the door – purposefully slowly, Harrison thought.

'I can't believe the incompetence. You have a murder suspect right under our noses because you didn't think to check on the eighth member of that group?'

'Sir, we were told he was dead, even DI Norman believed that...'

The rest of her explanation was lost to the incident room as the door slammed behind her.

Paige Nicholson lived in a large house outside the city borders. It was accessed by a short driveway, and Harrison estimated the gardens must be a good few acres. As he pulled up outside, the front door was opened by a petite, pretty blonde woman, who although she was nearly fifty, looked younger. Some subtle enhancements by a skilled cosmetic practitioner had worked to improve but not mask her natural good looks.

'Hello, detective,' Paige said holding out her hand to him.

'I'm not a detective; DS Fallon has been unfortunately detained back at the station, but my name is Dr Harrison Lane. I'm head of the Ritualistic Behavioural Crime unit.'

'Oh.' She looked a bit put out initially and then brightened. 'That sounds like an interesting title.' She peered at his ID. 'Come in. I've been so jumpy ever since poor Jordan was killed and when they phoned me to let me know about Ellie, well! What a terrible way to go. Been carrying the panic alarm button around with me ever since.'

The house was beautifully decorated and furnished. It was full of real antiques, and Harrison was reminded of Phil Stevenson's house, which was essentially a mock version of this but on a far smaller scale and without the genuine antiques.

'Lovely house,' Harrison said to her as they walked through into a large open-plan kitchen diner, which looked out through patio doors to a barbecue area and then big rolling lawns with an ornamental pond, and fields in the distance.

'Thanks. We've been here for about twenty-five years now. I met my husband straight after I graduated, he was actually my boss at work. We've had two children, our eldest is just in her second year at uni.'

'Do you still work?' Harrison asked, never knowing how to ask that question without it sounding like a judgemental one.

'No. Gave up when we had our firstborn, and just never went back. No need to financially thankfully, as you can see. My husband has his own consultancy business now and is just starting to wind down on the hours a bit. We've got a place in Italy that we plan to spend some time in. Would you like a coffee?'

Paige indicated an expensive coffee machine that looked like it should be operated by a barista.

'Just a glass of water, thank you.' He smiled.

Paige was quietly spoken with an understated nervous energy that made her appear like a frightened mouse at times. He could see why she had her admirers and with or without the help, age had not diminished her.

He started with the same questions they'd asked the other group members.

'Have you seen any of the others since the cave collapse thirty years ago?'

She shook her head. 'We went our own ways after that. It was a difficult time and the media attention spooked us all.

'Did you ever see Morgan?'

'No. His parents wouldn't let us anywhere near him. I wanted to go and see him, but then it was too late.'

Harrison didn't want to let Paige know that Morgan had in fact survived because it might impact the inquiry, but he had wanted to watch her reaction. She clearly believed he had died.

'Why did you agree to go back there two days ago? Weren't you nervous about going back after what had happened?'

'We're grown-ups now; we'd just been kids back then. It was a long time ago, you know!' she replied a little forcefully, and then softened again. 'Besides, Jordan said he had something to show us, and if I'm honest, I guess it was because I wanted to see how everyone had turned out.'

'Apart from what happened with Jordan, were there any surprises?'

'What you mean is, is everyone like I expected them to be?'

Harrison nodded.

'Yeah, pretty much. We're all older and wiser, but pretty much the same people. Dermot has changed the most. He seems to have become hippier in his old age. He used to be far more serious.'

'Is there a secret between you all, something you've kept hidden over the years? I'm asking because we're trying to find a motive.'

Paige hung her head and then looked out the window, before finally looking back at Harrison.

'We were scared. We'd been in a bit of a bubble, living out this belief that, somehow, we were going to be these amazing individuals who would rule the world. That came tumbling down with the rocks that fell on Morgan and Andy. What we'd been doing was totally harmless but it was obvious how people would view it and we weren't wrong, were we? The truth is that we didn't call for help immediately because we were so scared. That's been on my conscience for thirty years. Maybe Morgan could have been saved if we had.'

'Tell me about what you were doing, it was based on the Temple of Set, but how did you modify it?'

'There was nobody to guide us and show us what to do, so we just did our own thing.'

'You never met the man who Jordan got the information from?'

'No. It was someone back where he came from. We had the basics, that through the process of Xeper, you attempt to wilfully evolve into a God-like state. If I'm honest I can't say I ever really believed in it, but I don't know, somehow, we all got swept along by it. It was fun, we felt special because we were doing something that nobody else was doing, our secret. I swear to you that there wasn't anything like the newspapers made out. There was no sex or violence.'

'There was an inverse pentagram.' He nudged.

'Yes, it was the gateway to reach Set. Look, I know what you're thinking but seriously, it was no worse than kids doing a Ouija board or holding a seance, that kind of thing.'

'Did everyone feel like that?'

'What you mean is, did anyone take it more seriously?'

Harrison indicated that he did.

'Well, I'd say that Jordan and Phil were the most committed out of the boys, but Kelly was probably the most serious about it all. She'd get annoyed if one of us didn't give it the reverence, as she called it, that was needed. I think she thought she should lead it all really, not Jordan, even though it had been his idea. Morgan and Dermot just kind of followed along, as did Ellie and Andy and me.'

'Did you have your own names in the group?'

'Yes...' Paige looked a bit embarrassed. 'I was Tefnut, goddess of water; Andy was Nectanebus, the last native King of Egypt; Jordan was Ba-Pef, god of terror; Phil was Dedun, god of wealth; Morgan, Bes, god of music and merriment; Dermot, Ptah, god of art and craftsmen; Kelly, Seshat, goddess of writing, wisdom and knowledge; and Ellie, Nehebkau, snake god. All sounds a bit silly now, doesn't it, especially when you say it out loud.'

She looked at Harrison, who gave her a small sympathetic smile.

'I was goddess of water because I liked swimming. I used to go to the uni swim club, until we got more serious with our group.'

Harrison had written down all the names, some of which he had heard of, but there were a couple he hadn't. The fact that Ellie had been named after the snake god who, legend said, had swallowed seven cobras, couldn't be ignored.

Of all the group members, Paige was the most honest and open. He suspected that was because she felt secure in her family and in her life, and perhaps more remorseful than the others. They talked further about some of the rituals and spells that the group had performed, until Harrison needed to go in order to make the next appointment to meet Andy Lawson.

'Take care,' he said to her as he left. 'I fear that whoever killed Jordan and Ellie, and attempted to kill Andy, isn't finished yet.'

Her pupils dilated at his words, but Harrison felt no remorse for scaring her. Being on guard and vigilant could save her life.

TWENTY-ONE

DS Fallon met Harrison outside the cocktail bar owned by Andy Lawson.

'How'd it go with Paige Nicholson?' she asked and then added, 'We've still not tracked down Morgan.'

'Good, I'll fill you in after we've seen Mr Lawson.'

DS Fallon sighed and nodded. 'He's done alright for himself with this place. Got a reputation for being the trendy bar to be seen in. Mind you, one drink would probably cost me a week's salary.'

The bar did indeed look upmarket. It was stylishly decorated outside with what looked like stems of a flowering tree around the door, draped over the entrance. They were fake but didn't look tacky. When they walked in, a hostess in a smart black and white uniform came to greet them.

'Just drinks or something to eat?' she asked.

'Actually, we're here to see Mr Lawson, he should be expecting us,' the DS replied.

'No problem, please come this way.' The young woman smiled. Her accent was Eastern European, but her English was excellent.

'Please take a seat here and I'll go and find him for you,' she said, showing them to a table.

While she was gone, DS Fallon picked up the cocktail menu.

'I could do with a bloody drink,' she said, scanning the list of cocktails. 'Haven't heard of half of these though. All sorts of weird ingredients in them, look. Not a piña colada to be seen!'

She showed the list to Harrison who could have been reading Arabic for the sense it made to him. As a non-drinker, he very rarely looked at drinks lists. Even so, he could see some strange ingredients that, had he been guessing, he wouldn't have thought went in cocktails. There was one drink called *The Flaming Hell Pit* which showed an image of a cocktail on fire, another one called *Golden Burst* with vintage champagne, and cost £250; and the most expensive, the *Forever Yours* cocktail which contained a diamond – that cost £2,000. Others were all sorts of strange colours, some with what looked like white smoke rising from them, others with sparklers and flowers.

'Detectives, I see you've discovered our cocktail list. As you can see it's not just about the alcohol and the drink, we offer cocktails that are an experience here. It's more than just a G and T.' Andy Lawson's sales pitch tripped off his tongue.

'Indeed!' DS Fallon said as she watched two smoking cocktails go past her on a tray carried by a waiter.

'Thank you for agreeing to meet me here. I do apologise but we have an important supplier meeting later and quite frankly I'd rather be working and with people at the moment than sitting home alone after what happened and with all that's been going on.'

'Not a problem, Mr Lawson, we fully understand,' DS Fallon said, and introduced him to Harrison.

Andy Lawson was a fit man with a wiry build, blond hair and piercing blue eyes, but today he had dark circles under those eyes and looked exhausted. They exchanged handshakes – his was firm and businesslike.

'How have you been after your scare yesterday?'

'Have to say I didn't get much sleep, haven't really slept well since Jordan's murder. But like most people I'm terrified of snakes, especially the venomous kind. I know how close I came to getting bitten, one of them lunged but I just managed to knock the box to the floor and jump on the table to get myself out of the way. Horrible things.' Andy shook his head and looked away, remembering the encounter with the cobras.

'You've got a nice place here,' the DS said, indicating the bar and hoping to change the conversation and put him at ease.

'Thank you. I've worked hard for this. I'm thinking about opening up another one or two across the country. We're in *Vogue* this month, and I've got several Instagram and TikTok influencers raving about the place which is spreading the word. But we're not here to talk about my business,' Andy said, his face growing more serious. 'It's been a shocking week, first Jordan and then Ellie. Do you know who's doing this?'

'Not yet, but we are making progress,' the DS said. 'We're asking all members of the group if they know anyone who might want to do them harm. Was there anyone thirty years ago that was upset by what happened in that cave?'

'Bloody hell, it was a nightmare. Morgan's parents were certainly upset.'

'You were injured too, tell us what happened.'

'I have to be totally honest, Detective Fallon, and say that I don't actually remember too much. I never have. The doctors said that was quite a normal coping mechanism for anyone who has been in an accident like that. I vaguely remember being in the main cavern, but that's about all besides a flicker of falling rocks and the sound of them, like a wave coming in hard on a shingle beach.'

Harrison was watching Andy Lawson closely for any signs of stress as he retold the story.

'I got knocked out. When I came round it was pitch dark, there was dust and grit in my eyes, nose and mouth. I had stuff on top of me but I was able to push most of it away and crawled out of the rockfall. I had no idea Morgan was under it still. I couldn't see or hear the others and I couldn't even call out because I'd swallowed so much dust my throat was dried out. I passed out again halfway along the tunnel towards the exit and next time I woke up I was in hospital.'

'Must have been terrifying,' the DS said sympathetically.

'Can I ask you why you agreed to go back in there a few days ago? Didn't it bring back bad memories?' Harrison asked.

'Oh yes, and I wouldn't have been able to do it without the years of therapy. That fear of being trapped alone, of suffocating in dust, the darkness, it had far more impact on me psychologically than physically. The wonderful doctor Pieter Wagner has been a miracle worker. I suffered for years with full-blown night terrors, terrible broken sleep. I never felt rested and couldn't settle anywhere. Finally met a guy in Australia who'd been in the army and he told me about the symptoms he had, and that I was basically suffering from PTSD. Once I started researching it, I realised he was right and that's when I got help. I'm through it now though and I suppose that when I got that invitation, I felt like it was the final step in my recovery. Prove to myself that I could do it and come out unscathed. Never have to look back and feel scared again.'

'Had you seen any of the others before meeting that day?'

Andy shook his head. 'I was away travelling for a while after uni. That's when I learned my cocktail skills, working in some of the best bars and clubs in the world. New York, Singapore, Dubai. We kind of all went our own separate ways. I think you know about the stories in the media. That had a big impact on us all and we just wanted to distance ourselves from it and each other.'

'Did you believe in what you were doing?'

Andy smiled. 'I was young and impressionable. My first real foray away from a fairly strict home life. It was exciting and clandestine. We felt euphoric after our rituals, but of course it was all in our heads. You could argue that the principles of self-betterment were good lessons. I achieved this' – he gesticulated at the bar – 'because I worked hard and had the right attitude. I didn't need to do rituals and invoke an ancient Egyptian god to do it.'

'What about the others?' Harrison asked.

'Did they believe?' Andy thought a few moments. 'Look, I think we all did for a little while. We were an incestuous clique and it was all we talked about. The most serious about it all were Kelly and Jordan, they tended to direct the rituals, but we all took part – you had to. It wasn't about hanging on to the group's coattails; the whole point was that each of us did the work and so reached a higher level. Unfortunately for me, I got buried instead.'

'Some of the others say they heard a growling and saw mist coming from the tunnel the other day in the cave. Did you hear and see that?'

'Absolutely yes. We all heard it and we all saw it, no doubt at all.'

'What do you think it was?' Harrison asked.

'Well, I didn't know to be honest. I think I started to wonder if Jordan was playing a trick on us, some sick kind of joke.'

'It didn't frighten you at all bearing in mind what had happened last time?'

'It did concern me, yes, but I've got coping mechanisms I can employ when I feel stressed, and I'm still continuing my therapy. If it had been a rockfall then maybe I'd have gone over the top, but you know it all happened so fast that I don't think I had too much time to take it all in. We heard Jordan calling for help and went to see what we could do.'

'Mmm, about that... Are you sure it was Jordan who called out to you?' DS Fallon enquired.

'Well I think it was. It sounded like him, although obviously we hadn't heard his voice for thirty years. We weren't expecting anyone else to be there so naturally assumed.'

'Footsteps had been heard behind you though by Kelly, did you hear those?'

'I did.'

'So was it feasible that there was somebody else in the cave with you all?'

'Absolutely of course. Someone could easily have followed us in, how else did this all happen? We were all together all of the time.'

'But you never saw anybody else?'

'No, but the mist could have hidden them.' Andy looked at his watch and over at the bar where three people in business suits had gathered. 'I'm so sorry but I am going to have to go to this meeting now. You're welcome to stay for a drink, on the house, if you'd like. We do alcohol free if you're on duty.'

'Thank you, but we have work to do too. Just keep your guard up, Mr Lawson, anything unusual, you call us straight away.'

TWENTY-TWO

'Right, we've spoken to every one of the group now and I'm not sure I'm any closer to understanding what went on in that cave, either thirty years ago or two days ago. I just cannot think why someone has killed Jordan and Ellie and attempted to murder Andy – unless it is Morgan Grainger behind these murders and seeking revenge. Just wish we could track him down,' DS Fallon started her out-loud brainstorming. 'Either way I'm now too hungry to think about anything. Let's go get something to eat and you can tell me what Paige Nicholson said.'

Harrison wasn't a fan of dining out with work colleagues; he liked to go back to his room or home and allow the day's information to sink in so that he could process it. But there was no doubt that he too was hungry and as they both needed to eat and share information, it made sense.

They ended up in an Indian restaurant; it was convenient and had more than enough potential to fill the large holes in their stomachs.

DS Fallon ordered a chicken pasanda, while Harrison went for a jalfrezi; they both opted for poppadoms and dips as a shared starter.

'We've tracked Morgan up until about ten years ago and then he's fallen off the radar, so the team are going to keep working until they pick up the trail again,' the DS began.

'DS Fallon, can I ask you a question?' Harrison asked cautiously.

'Please call me Melinda,' she said.

'OK, likewise. Is the Detective Superintendent always like he was today?'

'Pretty much, yeah. It's why DI Chamberlain is on sick leave. Stress. He has a particular disdain for females.'

'Why do you put up with it?'

Melinda sighed and shook her head. 'It's not as easy as you think to complain about senior officers. I'm not going to let him break me.'

'You shouldn't have to put up with that,' Harrison said, genuinely concerned.

'Thanks, but I'm OK.'

'Well I hope your fiancé is supporting you. Mental health is as important as physical, I've seen some good officers buckle.'

At this point, she looked away from him and clenched her jaw.

For a moment Harrison thought she was angry, but then he saw tears brimming in her eyes.

'Apologies, I didn't mean to upset you,' he said.

She didn't reply immediately, keeping her eyes firmly fixed either to the left, right or in her lap as she wrestled with her emotions.

Harrison gave her some time, mindful not to pressurise her. He thought about his good friend Detective Chief Inspector Sandra Barker.

'I know a good female DCI who would be more than happy to talk to you, she's had to deal with misogyny along the way.'

Melinda shook her head and gave a shuddering sigh before pulling herself together and looking directly at Harrison.

'Thank you, but it's not that. It's my fiancé. He died eight months ago. A brain tumour. He was thirty-five. We were due to be married next month and I really miss him.'

Her chin crumpled and she looked away again. 'It destroyed me when he died, it's only when the person you love gets given a death sentence and then you lose them, that you realise just how much their love meant. I'd been working such long hours and when we got the results, he literally only had weeks to live. I took time off work, which didn't go down too well with Smith, but it's harder when you're not married. I didn't get to make the decisions after he'd passed, his parents did. Things he'd told me about what he wanted after he'd gone, I couldn't do for him.'

She looked at Harrison. 'Don't get me wrong, his parents have been great with me, but once he was gone, that was it. All I have left are photographs and a grave that he didn't want. Although I know it was tough for his parents and funerals are for the living, right? So you see, whatever Smith throws at me is nothing compared to that.' She said it all quickly, forcing the words out.

Harrison stared into her tear-filled eyes and saw what she worked so hard to hide: a deep well of loneliness and loss.

'I'm so sorry,' he said.

'Do you have a partner?' Melinda asked, her eyes glancing towards his wedding band finger.

'I...' Harrison paused a moment, a tsunami of Tanya images and feelings hitting him. 'We're on a time-out break at the moment.'

'Oh OK.' Melinda searched his face. 'Do you mind me asking, was it your decision?'

Harrison felt awkward in the face of someone whose love was so clearly raw and unconditional. 'It was me, but she agreed it was a good idea.'

Melinda nodded thoughtfully but said nothing in response at first.

'You know I loved him, and he loved me, but he wasn't perfect. I'm not. Our relationship wasn't perfect either. That's just in Hollywood. Don't wait for the perfect set of circumstances. I know it's hurting now, but I wouldn't have missed the time we had together for anything.'

Harrison wasn't sure what to say. He suspected that Melinda was more intuitive than he'd given her credit for. Either way, he was saved by the waiter arriving with the poppadoms and sauces and for a moment they focused on rearranging drinks and plates on the table.

'So, tell me, what did you think of Paige Nicholson?' Melinda asked. The mask was back on and it was clear the previous conversation was over. Harrison hesitated, but felt he should respect her wishes and steered back to talking about the case.

'She was straight with me. Told me more about the rituals and mechanisms of their group than all the others have.'

'And? Were they the satanic students that old Ron reckoned they were, do you think?'

'Yes and no. The Temple of Set is an offshoot of the Church of Satan, and they believe Set is the original prince of darkness. And they are probably right too.'

'Really? How comes?'

'The name Satan comes from Hebrew, and meant opposer or adversary, which was how Set became known in Egypt. The Old Testament was written as early as 1200 BC, but Set was already in existence in Egyptian religions and mythology as early as 3000 years BC. So technically, they were Satanists.'

Melinda nodded her understanding.

'Like you said about the wax dolls, lots of people took on the Egyptian beliefs in the years after?'

'Exactly, yes. The Hebrews and Greeks, and indeed other pagan beliefs, took many of the Egyptian religious practices and made them their own, modifying them, and ultimately so did Christianity.'

'Religious recycling.' Melinda smiled, chomping on a poppadom.

'Yes, you can see it in Christianity. They took the Hebrew Bible forward and created the New Testament about fifty years or so after Jesus had died. They also took on pagan celebrations and turned them into their own, such as what we call Halloween, was originally a Pagan celebration and then became All Souls Day; and of course Christmas was invented by the Romans to take over the pagan holiday of Saturnalia following the winter solstice. So, in that way, yes there is a strong link with what we know as our modern Satan, but it is less about evil and debauchery and more about following the left-hand path.'

Melinda stopped crunching and looked at Harrison to show she needed an explanation.

'Set or Satan is about the left-hand path, spiritualism and independent thinking, whereas the right-hand path is seen as following the path of order and union with god or an authoritarian religion.'

'OK, so it all goes back to the Egyptians, but how does this relate to our former students?'

'When you ask me were the students satanic, I would say not in the way that the label was meant. I don't think there was any of the kind of lurid goings on that you hear associated with satanic rituals and cults in popular culture. It was an alternative kind of student fraternity. They took the basic initiation information of the Temple and then modified it to suit their own aims. I can't be one hundred per cent sure, but I don't think there was anything too controversial going on.' Harrison dipped his poppadom into some mango chutney and scooped up some onion with it. 'Although that's not to say that I don't think they have any secrets. I think there is something they're hiding, just not the satanic cult that Ron Norman would have us believing.'

'It's interesting to know all that background.' She was quiet for a moment, thinking. 'You didn't mention Morgan to her, did you?' the DS suddenly asked.

'No.'

'Good. If we get any kind of indication that he could be in the area then we'll need to let them all known then, but I don't want to panic them that a ghost is coming back to seek revenge; or potentially give him a heads-up that we're onto him.'

Harrison smiled.

'So do you think that there really was a growling in that cave and mist? Or was it all in their minds?'

'Obviously again I can't be one hundred per cent sure, but I think yes there was a growling and I think the mist was also used to induce fear and hide whatever it was that had made the noise.'

DS Fallon raised her eyebrows to encourage him to continue.

'Every one of them that we have spoken to looked to me to totally believe what they were saying. Now that's no guarantee that something was real – we can believe something because our minds interpret events in a certain way. And in a group once one person has suggested something, it's often the case that the other group members will adopt that same view.'

'It's the same principles we learn when in interview training. Keep witnesses separate so that one person's perspective doesn't influence the others.'

'That's right, but it would have been easy to place some kind of audio device in that tunnel, there are plenty of rock ledges. It could then have automatically played growling sounds, and perhaps even footsteps. The natural acoustics of the rock in the tunnel, funnelling the noise into the chamber, would have amplified it. When they ran back through after Jordan had been killed, the mist and their panic would have ensured they didn't see a device. The killer could have then gone and picked it up before anyone else arrived, removing all evidence.'

'Why go to all that trouble?'

'They clearly wanted to unnerve the group, terrify them. Perhaps it served to also make sure they went forward into the smaller chamber and not just run out the cave straight away, which would have defeated their plans for Jordan.'

'But why all the theatrics and why kill Jordan in that way?'

'They wanted to frighten and scare both the whole group and Jordan. They all spoke about the terror in his eyes behind the Set mask. He was their leader and as they came to rescue him, they set off the weapon which killed him. It's highly symbolic.'

With that Harrison took another bite of his poppadom and looked at the woman in front of him, who reminded him just a little of another woman, whom he hadn't seen for nearly two months. Tanya. In that moment, witnessing Melinda's raw grief for the loss of her partner, he'd realised just how big a hole not seeing Tanya had left in his life. No matter how much he'd tried to throw himself into his work. No matter how often he'd told himself it was the best thing for her and for him, he could never fully convince himself that he didn't love her.

The question was, had he left it too late for her to ever consider taking him back?

TWENTY-THREE

Kelly Watts had come back to her flat after the police interview so that she could work from home for the rest of the afternoon. She liked to be in the office in the morning to deal with her staff and any issues with clients, and then have the afternoon to work in peace and quiet without being disturbed. Today was no exception.

One of the women at work had announced her engagement and there'd been all sorts of chattering and squawking from the rest of her co-workers which Kelly just couldn't deal with. Why it was such a big deal she didn't know. They'd been living together for years and neither of them attended any church. All the talk of wedding dresses and honeymoons had nearly given her a headache. Coming home was a very welcome respite.

She followed the same routine every day. Get home at lunchtime, take off her work clothes and change into something more relaxing. Make a cup of tea and a sandwich, have ten minutes and then be at her computer by 1.30 p.m. She didn't like to deviate from that routine; if she did, it slightly set her on edge. She had to have absolute streamlined control of everything in her life because that's the way she had become successful. Those early rituals where they'd followed the philosophy of the Temple of Set had established her life for success. She earned more than anyone she knew and she could lacerate a business opponent in seconds. She had more drive and focus than all her team put together and she made sure they knew it.

She had just made herself a cheese and tomato sandwich and started her ten-minute break when the doorbell rang.

Who the hell was that?

Kelly stomped to the front door and peered through the spy hole. Outside was a man in full white forensic suit with a mask and hood.

'What do you want?' she shouted at him through the door.

'I'm sorry, is this Kelly Watt's flat? I've been asked by Detective Sergeant Fallon to come round and pick up the clothes you were wearing at the cave the other day. I'm part of the forensic team looking into Jordan Oaks's murder.'

Kelly swore under her breath.

'Why didn't she tell me this, I've not long since seen her?'

The man held his hands up as if in surrender. 'I'm sorry, I'm just doing my job. She's pretty busy. Do you want to see my ID?'

Kelly looked at her watch. As if she wasn't busy too! Her ten minutes was up: she should be at her desk by now. Quickly she unbolted the front door and opened it.

'Can we hurry up with this. I have work to do.'

'Certainly,' he said picking up his black rucksack and holding a big plastic bag ready to receive her clothes. 'This shouldn't take more than a minute. If you can get the clothes, and do you have the shoes you wore too?'

Kelly turned back around and went into her bedroom to find her clothes as she heard the front door close. She swore at his cheek. She'd not asked him into the flat, purposely left him standing outside.

She was just bending down to pick up the shoes when the man came into the bedroom after her.

'You can wait in the hall!' she said to him sharply.

But the man didn't stop or turn around, instead he came straight for her.

She had no time to react.

Her brain registered the flash of something metallic and then she felt a searing pain in her left eye. She made to scream, but he was right in front of her and something was shoved into her mouth. Whatever was in her eye was rammed in harder. She fell backwards against the wardrobe, crashing down. Her hands scrabbling to try to get whatever it was in her eye out, choking on the object in her mouth.

Blind panic as there was another searing pain and something entered at her throat, bursting through her windpipe.

Kelly was on her back suffocating in her own blood – mortally wounded and unable to fight off the man who now loomed over her.

Her one good eye stared into the eyes of the killer as they leant over her ready to strike again, and the realisation struck. She knew who it was. But why?

It made no difference. The knowledge that she had wouldn't ever be of any use to her or anyone else because she'd never get the chance to share it.

Mercifully for Kelly Watts, she blacked out.

TWENTY-FOUR

After his curry, Harrison had returned to the hotel feeling tired and full. There was clearly no chance he could exercise after eating like that and so instead he'd gone to his room and called Ryan to see if he'd got any updates for him.

'Boss!' Ryan answered.

Harrison could instantly tell that something was up.

'Everything OK?'

'Yeah sure. All good,' Ryan replied but his eyes kept shifting off to the right.

'You alone?'

'Yeah, course.'

'Lucy not visiting then?'

This was their way of ensuring that Ryan wasn't under duress.

'No. Really, there's no one here and you and I both know that Lucy is fake.'

Harrison relaxed a little, at least there was nobody in Ryan's flat threatening him, but he was still convinced that something was up.

'So what you got for me?'

'Right, nothing much on any of them, although Phil Stevenson has money troubles. Seems he's overstretched himself and is in a bit of a debt spiral. No County Court Judgements, so it's not going to flag up straight away, but won't be long before he's going to be in hot water unless he does something.'

'That's interesting but it fits with his character. He didn't grow up with much and wanted to be the big man in the big house. Not sure how this would make him the killer though, unless he blames the group for the fact their magic didn't work.'

'It's possible,' Ryan said distractedly.

'Have I interrupted something?' Harrison tried again.

'No you're fine. Andy Lawson seems to be a success story, his bars are doing well, and so too is Kelly Watt's business. Paige's husband is loaded, made his money in furniture. The society drop-out is Dermot O'Connelly, who has gone from a well-paid job in the legal profession to occasional walking guide and whatever else he does on the side and under the radar. No convictions, but definitely on the edges.'

'Yes, not a fan of capitalism and rule books, perhaps he bears a grudge or thinks the others have all betrayed the original group ethos.'

'Mmm,' Ryan replied, not even looking at his laptop camera and Harrison.

'Ryan, is everything OK with the flat?'

'Absolutely, yes, although...' Ryan thought for a moment, 'you know I've been thinking about maybe moving out of London, going somewhere that I can have a garden, you know?'

'Garden? Really? That's a great idea. Harrison knew that Ryan's agoraphobia usually meant stepping outside was more stressful than enjoyable so for him to be suggesting a garden was a huge step forward. 'Things been going well with the therapist then?'

Before Ryan could answer something passed across the screen.

For a moment Harrison couldn't work out what it was.

'What was that?'

Ryan looked a little panicked.

Then it passed back again and this time Harrison could see that it was a thin grey fluffy tail with a white tip.

'Ryan?'

Ryan looked wide-eyed back at the screen.

'It was my neighbour,' he began.

'Neighbour! That doesn't look like a neighbour.'

'No, I mean, she brought her round, asked me to look after her as she had to go away for a couple of days, only I think she's gone. The landlord came round not long after, changed the locks on the door and they've cleaned the flat out. So I couldn't just dump her, could I?'

Just then the little kitten clambered up Ryan's chest and snuggled into him. Despite worrying about the reaction of his boss, Ryan couldn't help nestling his chin into her head in response. When he looked up, Harrison was smiling.

'Looks like she's adopted you and made herself at home.'

Ryan's shoulders seemed to drop six inches and he let out a sigh of relief.

'She has. I'm not supposed to have pets here though and there's nowhere for her to go outside.'

'Don't worry, Ryan, we can sort it. Looks like you're enjoying her company.'

'I am.' He looked at Harrison like a child trying to persuade his parents to let him keep something.

'I thought you never wanted pets.'

'I didn't. Didn't want the responsibility or have to face losing it. There was a cat once, when I was little, but you know my mother.'

Harrison did know Ryan's mother. She'd been a drug addict

for most of his life and that meant everything else, including him, had come second to the need to get her next fix.

'We struggled to have enough money to feed her. She got thinner and thinner. I even used to bring home some of my school lunch. One day I came home from school and she was in the road, a car had hit her. I think she died straight away but Mum didn't even care. Said she'd seen her already when I told her. I buried her in the garden on my own. It was hard. She'd been a loving little cat. She hadn't deserved what happened to her. It hurt losing her which is why I guess I never wanted another pet.' Ryan looked down at the kitten. 'But this little one has no one else, she needs me and I'm enjoying having her here.'

Harrison thought about Melinda Fallon and what she'd said earlier about not wanting to have missed the time she'd spent with her fiancé, despite the pain she was feeling now.

'Well, there's no reason that you have to live in London and maybe it's better that you don't. Get away from the gang that you keep worrying you might bump into again. Perhaps that kitten coming along is just what you needed. When I'm back we can look at the options for moving.'

Ryan beamed at him and stroked the little kitten who was looking as though she was about to fall asleep on his chest.

The sight of Ryan so content with the cat made Harrison smile too – inside and out. That something so small could bring such joy was incredible. Then he remembered the old dog that had adopted his family in America, and the day he had disappeared again. Harrison had found him being eaten by the buzzards. He didn't want Ryan to go through that heartbreak again so they'd have to find a place well away from any big roads for him and the kitten to live.

'What's her name?'

'Well, she didn't come with one, so I've named her.' Ryan said looking pleased with himself. 'Arwen.'

'Unusual name.'

'She's a character in *Lord of the Rings*.'

'Should have known.' Harrison smiled.

'I've ordered her a nice bed and some toys, and some food. They say that she needs stimulation too so I'm playing with her and training her. I've no idea how old she is but she only looks little.'

'She's a very lucky cat,' Harrison said and he meant it. Ryan had never had anyone to love or to love him back. With his mother's first priority being drugs that resulted in him coming a very poor second. His agoraphobia meant Ryan found it nearly impossible to make friends, let alone get a girlfriend. The kitten would be a wonderful addition – and might even get him outside in his new garden once they'd moved. Perhaps even be the first steps to a full recovery.

Ryan had a permanent smile on his face for the rest of the conversation, but then stopped.

'Have you heard from Tanya?' he asked.

'Not lately,' Harrison tried to sound nonchalant but failed.

'You know she's thinking about leaving and going travelling for a while?'

'Tanya? Travelling? But she loves her job.'

Ryan nodded and shrugged. He looked at his boss's face on the screen.

Harrison said nothing more. A lump had appeared in his throat and chest. A small lump that grew with every second he contemplated never seeing Tanya ever again. He'd been in denial, he knew it, but he'd been fighting it ever since that day in his flat when he'd failed to show her any commitment. For weeks he'd been trying to persuade himself that it was in her best interests if she found someone else, but that thought made him sick to the core.

· · ·

Harrison fell asleep feeling as though he'd experienced a loss. He couldn't remember his dreams but they were heavy on his mind and he woke with a jolt at his alarm on his phone. There was already a text in from Melinda Fallon which made him sit up and wake up.

> Morgan found. Living in Melbourne, Australia. Arranged video call for 8 a.m.

That was both good and bad news for the inquiry. It meant they could now discount him, but it left the field wide open again in terms of suspects. Harrison quickly got showered and dressed and headed straight into the incident room. After yesterday's curry, he decided to skip breakfast and fast until at least dinner time. Endless cooked hotel breakfasts weren't going to help his arteries.

DS Fallon was at her desk looking pale and tired.

'Well, that's one theory out the window,' she said to him. 'He's not been to the UK for about five years, not since his mother died. Our ghost is not the killer.' She gave a big sigh. 'We still don't have a clear motive, or even the suggestion of a suspect – unless he's hired a hitman or it's somehow one of the group members themselves.'

'There's no reason why it couldn't be one of the group,' Harrison said. 'Everything was set up prior to them all being there. We've not considered them seriously because they'd all heard footsteps behind them suggesting a third party, and they'd all been together, but what if that was an audio recording like the growling? It's perfectly feasible.'

'You're right. But first, let's go and talk to the ghost man and see if he can throw any light on this.'

Morgan Grainger's suntanned face filled the screen in the small meeting room. DS Fallon, one of her detectives, Richard

Donning, and Harrison, were sat around the small table looking towards the end where a video conference camera captured them; and the screen showed Morgan in a home office with the last of the Melbourne daylight coming through a side window.

'This is totally out of the blue,' Morgan said as they introduced themselves. 'Haven't thought about all this stuff for years.'

'I'm sorry to dig it all up again, Mr Grainger, but we have a major murder inquiry underway and we had presumed that you died thirty years ago, which we've since learned didn't happen. That incident could be related to these murders.'

'Nothing to do with me, I can tell you that much,' Morgan asserted. 'My parents were horrified when it all came out. They'd been brought up Catholics, you know, and when the press started calling us satanic and all that crap got written up about what we were supposed to have been up to... well you can imagine that it didn't go down too well with them.'

'Can you talk us through how you became involved in the group and what happened at the end?'

'Sure, what I remember of it all. When I got to uni I found myself in halls with the others. There were eight of us in the one unit. We shared a kitchen and a bathroom between us. Had to slum it in those days, my son has a nice en suite where he is. Anyway, we were all thrust together, all freshers and trying to find our feet together. Then one night we went down the pub and Jordan started talking about this group and how it could help us improve our intelligence and become successful in life. It's like the promise of a lottery, isn't it? Sounded great and made the rest of us think that if we weren't in it then we were going to miss out. So we all joined in and it became a bit of an obsession.'

'So, Jordan was the initiator?' DS Fallon clarified.

'Yeah, if I remember rightly, Jordan had got the information off a friend from home.'

DS Fallon nodded and Morgan took that as his cue to continue.

'It went on for most of the rest of that year. We had red, hooded cloaks made, which we used to keep at the cave for our most important rituals. Didn't always do them there. We did a fair few smaller ones in the halls. We made a silver circled pentagram – that was the gateway. Had one in the cave and one at home. We read loads of stuff about improving ourselves, reaching a higher level of spirituality and all that stuff. There were no orgies and no sacrifices like the papers said.'

'What about the paintings in the cave?'

'Oh yeah, they were rabbit's blood but we didn't kill it. We found it when we were walking up to the cave one day. Some bird of prey must have just got it and we disturbed it. It was still warm. So Phil got this idea of using its blood to draw Set's name on the cave walls. Said it was put there for us to do that. I didn't feel that comfortable with it, but it was dead anyways, so...' Morgan shrugged.

'Who would you say was the most into the group?'

'Oh that would be Kelly for sure – and Phil. He was desperate to make money and get rich. Thought this might be the answer. Kelly, I think, just liked the whole structure of it all.'

'What happened on the day of the accident?'

'I don't remember a huge amount to be honest – I don't know whether it's a coping mechanism or a physical symptom, but I can't remember the rockfall at all. I know that we hadn't been to the cave for a while. It had been raining a lot and some of us were losing our interest in the group a bit. It was getting a bit tedious and Jordan and Kelly seemed to think they were in charge of us all because they were leader and deputy leader. I don't even remember what we called them now. Anyway, we went that day and it was very wet in the cave, I guess that must have caused the rockfall. We went into the main chamber, conducted a ritual, and were still in our cloaks when we heard rocks falling. I just remember running, trying to get out, and that's it.'

'You said some of you were losing interest, who exactly?' Harrison leant forward in his chair, interested.

'So, Phil was a bit miffed that although he'd been one of the original starters, he'd been kind of pushed out the leadership circle. He was stirring it a bit. Paige just went along with whatever the majority said, but Dermot, Andy and I, we were getting bored and didn't feel like we were getting anywhere. Kelly had gradually made it all really serious, probably more so than Jordan would have done if left to his own devices. I think even if the rockfall hadn't happened, the group would have fallen apart. It was the end of the first year and some of us were thinking about moving in with other people rather than all staying together.'

'Did Jordan and Kelly know this?'

'Yeah, I think they got the vibe.'

'Is there anyone who you can think might be angry or upset at what went on, who might be seeking revenge now?'

Morgan thought hard, but slowly shook his head.

'No. We didn't hurt anyone. I know my parents went ballistic about it all and they were really annoyed when the police dropped the case against the others, but I was glad it didn't amount to anything. I just wanted to move on. They insisted that I moved uni and sent me over here to get me as far away as possible from the others. Bit of overkill but I didn't complain: guaranteed sunshine, surf and non-stop barbies, turned out to be a bit more of an attraction than wet, dull Leeds. But there was nobody else involved. I can't understand who would be doing this and why.'

'Great,' DS Fallon said, scrubbing at her face with her hands and then running through her hair absent-mindedly after they'd finished the video call. 'In some ways that was informative, but in others it puts us right back to square one. No reason why anyone would want to be killing off the group members.'

'Well someone thinks they have a reason,' Harrison said to her. 'It's perhaps lain dormant for a long time, but there's a deep-seated hatred in them, and something had triggered it. Question is, who and what?'

TWENTY-FIVE

Visiting the family of a victim is never an easy task and when it's an elderly parent it can be all the more harrowing. Jordan Oaks's mother was frail and broken. She looked like a small branch of a tree that had been snapped off and left to dry out. The life had gone out of her eyes and Harrison and DS Fallon felt the weight of responsibility on their shoulders.

'It should be me who's dead, not him. You're supposed to go before your children. I don't have long left, but Jordan was happy and still had his life to live.'

Mrs Oaks had a small ground-floor flat in an over fifty-fives complex. She had used a walker aid to let them in and to return to her chair.

'Would you like a cup of tea?' she'd asked them both.

Neither had said yes, not wanting to trouble her further.

'We are very sorry for your loss, Mrs Oaks,' Melinda had said gently.

Her only response was a tiny nod of her head. What could she say? There was no one sorrier than her.

'Who did this to my boy?' she asked, opaque eyes settling on first DS Fallon and then Harrison. 'It wasn't one of those right-wing, phobic people, was it?'

They both knew that his mother was referring to Jordan's choice of partners.

'No we don't believe it was a hate crime, Mrs Oaks. We think it may link back to Jordan's time at university.'

'That was decades ago.'

'Yes, thirty years since there was the accident in the cave, but somebody invited Jordan and the rest of the group back to that same cave. We wanted to ask you about back then, how Jordan got involved in the Set religion?'

Mrs Oaks sighed, collapsing back further into the armchair and looking out the window to the little patio area she had outside. A couple of sparrows were pecking at a bird feeder while their friends were on the ground hoovering up the spillage.

'It hadn't been an easy time at home. His dad and I weren't getting on, mostly money troubles. My husband had lost his job and he was a proud man so that had a big impact on him.' She looked to a photograph on the wall. An elderly man was smiling back at them. 'We sorted things out and he got another job, but for a couple of years things were tough. He was hard on Jordan too – it was becoming apparent that our son liked boys not girls, and it took a little while for my husband to come round and realise that it didn't matter. He was still our son. It just wasn't so accepted then as it is now.'

She looked at them for understanding and they both smiled and nodded.

'He knew his dad was proud of him. Richard passed six years ago. They spoke on the phone every week.' Mrs Oaks's eyes grew watery and she brushed at them, her age-spotted hands pulling her sagging skin.

DS Fallon gave her a moment.

'Is Jordan your only child?'

'Yes,' she whispered back.

'Back thirty years ago, Mrs Oaks, we understand that there was someone who introduced Jordan to the Set religion?'

The elderly woman in front of them scowled. 'That was Paul Iverson, he was always a wrong one. A couple of years older than Jordan. Got excluded from school if I remember. Was into all sorts. The whole family are trouble. Paul had gone to America. Don't ask me how he'd got the money for that, but he had. Came back a few months before Jordan was due to go to Leeds. Jordan had finished his exams and had several months holiday which meant that apart from a part-time job, he was around the house a lot. That's when he and his dad were clashing so he used to take himself out. He and Paul started hanging around together. I caught them smoking dope one day, had to keep him out of the way of his father. Anyway, it was Paul who gave him that Egyptian cult nonsense.'

'Does Paul still live around here?'

'He got locked up years ago. Drugs and burglary and the like. No idea where they put him but you lot took him off the streets, thank goodness.'

'OK, thank you, that's useful. Was there anyone else involved with Paul and Jordan at that time?'

Mrs Oaks shook her head.

'Can I ask, were you still talking to Jordan regularly?' Harrison queried.

'Yes. Every Sunday evening he would call me.' She shook her head and tried to hold back the tears.

'Did Jordan mention the other students from Leeds at all? There were eight of them who were friends – had any of them got in touch?'

'No. After what happened in the cave, they didn't really stay friends. It was a shock to him, but he sorted himself out. Got a first in his degree, you know.'

'And Jordan didn't leave anything with you for safekeeping, nothing like that?' DS Fallon asked.

'No. I moved from our family home after my husband passed. Jordan helped me sort things out and took anything that was his. If you're meaning anything to do with that Egyptian nonsense, he got rid of all that thirty years ago.'

'Thank you for your time, Mrs Oaks, we won't keep you any longer.'

The elderly woman looked exhausted.

'Please don't get up, we can see ourselves out.'

'Find them, will you? And soon. I don't have long but I shan't rest until I know who did this to my boy and that they're receiving the justice they deserve.'

DS Fallon let out a big sigh as they walked back through the estate to the car park.

'No pressure then. I'd much rather have the Detective Superintendent on my back and conscience than Mrs Oaks. That poor woman.'

Harrison didn't need to reply, she knew he agreed.

'I'll get the team onto tracking down where Paul Iverson is. I'd like to have a word with him about what went on thirty years ago and what exactly it was that he passed on to Jordan.'

TWENTY-SIX

Harrison was standing in a motorway service station, staring out the window, oblivious to the flow of people around him, and thinking about the group and who might want to hurt them. The multi-coloured, multi-sized British public oozed in through the automatic doors heading to toilets and food outlets; while their doppelgänger counterparts, watered, fed, and suitably relieved, trickled out. Some dragged reluctant children who'd been caught by the bright lights of the arcade, others simply trudged back to their cars and the inevitable mind-numbing motorway drive to wherever their final destinations lay.

Could Paul Iverson be the killer? He had more than enough form, but Harrison was dubious. From his record, the crimes hadn't involved much intelligence and were purely self-motivated. What would a man like Iverson gain from killing Jordan Oaks? The only other obvious explanation is that it was one of the group themselves, but he still couldn't see the motive. Jealousy about status and money could be a contender, but these people hadn't seen each other for decades so why now, and what could be so deep-rooted that it took thirty years to seek revenge?

'Harrison!' DS Fallon called him from behind.

He turned to see her looking pale and tense.

'We need to go. Kelly Watts's office has called, they can't raise her and it's extremely unlike her not to be in work on time. We've sent someone round to her flat and there's no answer, but they can hear her mobile ringing out inside. I've got a team ready to get in there if we don't hear from her within the time it takes to get to the flat.'

Harrison's heart sank. Surely not another one?

DS Fallon's driving on an empty stomach left a little to be desired, but mercifully the journey wasn't too long. They pulled up outside a block of expensive executive-looking flats that were now sullied by a fringe of emergency vehicles parked on the double yellow lines outside.

'Nice place,' Melinda said, 'must cost a packet but at least it should mean we'll get some CCTV footage if our worst fears are realised.' She nodded at the security cameras.

As DS Fallon got out, a van disgorged four tactical support officers in protective gear, one of whom held a battering ram. DS Fallon pressed the entrance buzzer to be let in, and Harrison hung behind, letting the operational team go first.

'Hello,' a voice said.

'Police, can you let us in please.'

'Wait there, I'll need to see ID.'

They stood waiting for a couple of minutes before a man appeared and peered through the glass door. DS Fallon showed her ID and he buzzed it open.

'Do you work here?' she asked.

He nodded. 'I'm caretaker, live on site.'

'So do you have access to all the flats?'

'Have you got a warrant?'

'No. We have reason to believe that Kelly Watts's life is in danger and we need to access her flat.'

His eyes widened.

'Ms Watts, she won't be happy with me if I let you into her place.'

'She won't be happy with you if she's still alive in there, and we can get her some medical treatment. She hasn't gone into work today and we have enough reason to think that someone might be wishing her harm. Do you understand?'

He thought about it for a few more moments.

'It's a simple choice, we either break the door down and make a big mess, or you open it with your key.'

That was enough – he nodded.

'You're going to have to explain it to her though. I don't wanna lose my job here.'

A few minutes later all seven of them were outside the penthouse flat door, together with two uniformed officers who had been the first to report that Kelly Watts wasn't answering her door. The nine of them crowded along the small strip of corridor.

DS Fallon knocked on the door. 'Ms Watts, it's the police.' The line of officers listened silently and the caretaker looked as though he was holding his breath. 'Ms Watts, it's DS Fallon. If you don't answer this door, I am going to have to force entry.'

Silence.

'OK.' DS Fallon nodded the caretaker forward, who went to put a key in the lock.

'Thank you, but we'll take it from here,' she said to him. She'd put forensic overshoes on ready to go inside.

The caretaker didn't look overly convinced.

'It could be dangerous so we need to secure the area.'

Two of the tactical support officers moved in behind the

DS, ready to help. The caretaker, a skinny man who didn't look like he'd visited a gym in his life, sensibly dropped back.

'Over here, sir, please,' one of the uniformed officers said to him, and the caretaker found himself at the back of the queue, behind Harrison.

DS Fallon stood to one side of the doorway, as did the others, all well trained to know that you never opened doorways face-on. With her gloved hands, she turned the key and handle and pushed the door open, trying to touch as little as possible.

DS Fallon peered around the doorframe.

'Ms Watts! Ms Watts, are you here? It's DS Fallon, the police.' She paused on the threshold, listening and looked down at the floor where a trail of blood led along its length. 'Call an ambulance and get forensics down here now,' she said to one of the officers. 'Ms Watts, we're coming in.'

The two tactical officers stepped inside first, tasers at the ready.

'Careful. We've had booby-trapped devices and poisonous snakes already, so tread cautiously,' she said to them as they entered. She followed close behind.

Harrison waited outside while they made the initial sweep of the flat, out of protocol rather than choice. It didn't take long for DS Fallon and the two who'd accompanied her to reappear. She looked even paler than earlier and dry retched as she exited. One of the officers wasn't so lucky, he threw up outside the lift, much to the disgust of the caretaker.

'No need for an ambulance,' she said to Harrison and the rest of the team. 'We just need someone to certify death.'

DS Fallon turned to the caretaker. 'I need you to leave this area, but one of my officers is going to come with you. I want every second of CCTV footage that you have in and around this building in the last twenty-four hours. There will be more personnel arriving, so please make sure they can get in.'

'What do I tell the other residents?' the caretaker said as the enormity of what was going on sunk in.

'Nothing. You don't need to tell them anything. It's a targeted crime so they're not in any danger.'

DS Fallon nodded to one of the uniformed officers who guided the stunned caretaker away. Just as he was going, another thought occurred to her.

'Did you let anyone else into this flat?'

He shook his head quickly.

'It is very important that you tell me if you did, even if they paid you, because your life could be in danger if that is the case.'

'No. Nobody. I'm an honest man. I don't let people into my residents' flats. Never.'

'And do you know if anyone else has a key? Does she have a cleaner come in?'

He shook his head. 'I've never seen anyone else.'

She believed him and nodded that he could go.

DS Fallon took a few breaths and then turned to Harrison.

'I need you to go in there and tell me what the hell is going on, what it means. But it's not pretty. Just to warn you. Full forensic suit please.'

She turned to the other officers. 'Once Dr Lane's come out, I want this flat sealed off until Eric and his team have been in.'

Harrison suspected he was going to be thankful that he hadn't eaten that morning after all.

Once he was fully suited, Harrison walked into the hallway of Kelly Watt's flat. Melinda had already told him that she was in the kitchen, and yet there was a blood trail from a room on the right. He pushed the door and stepped inside a bedroom.

Harrison stood for a moment and closed his eyes, focusing his mind. What had gone on here? There was no damage to the front door so she must have let her assailant in. They'd attacked her in here. Blood spurt patterns showed that she'd been near the wardrobe when she'd been stabbed. A smear of red was on the mirrored door. Shoes were knocked off a rack. Bloody finger marks were visible. She must have fought for her life.

What weapon had been used? Why would she have let her assailant in – was it someone she knew or a delivery person? Had she gone into the bedroom for a reason, or had she run in, panicked and they'd followed her in here?

The blood was dried, dark crimson brown and not its fresh, oxidised red. The attack hadn't happened that morning. He thought back to their interview with her yesterday. She'd said she worked from home in the afternoons. A creature of habit. That habit may have helped seal her fate.

He looked around at her bedroom. The most private place in her life. It reflected her personality. Stark white walls. No clutter. The wardrobe, apart from the disturbed shoe rack, was immaculately tidy. He crossed to the bed and looked in the two small cabinets on either side. One contained a book on productivity, along with some hand cream and a pair of reading glasses. The other one was empty.

Harrison followed the trail of blood to where he knew the killer had taken the body. It indicated that she'd been dragged down the hall and through the living room area, quite probably when she was alive because of the amount of blood that had been gushing out of her.

He stopped in the living room for a moment, taking in Kelly Watts's possessions. It was clear that despite thirty years passing, she still held some belief in the power of Set. There was a statue of him on a bookcase, along with a silver inverted pentagram. Had she still carried out rituals, or were these simple talismans that she might occasionally tip a nod to? He'd have to do a more detailed search to answer that question and right now he couldn't until forensics had been in and combed the place.

Instead, he returned to the blood trail and followed its inevitable end.

In the kitchen he found her laid out on the kitchen floor. Her body looked almost dumped, as though it wasn't important.

As Harrison got closer, he saw the pools of blood that had oozed onto the white tiled floor. There was a partial trainer print – it had to be the killer's.

He didn't want to disturb the blood or slip in it and he didn't need to get closer than a few feet. From where he stood, he could see the message that the killer had left.

Kelly Watts's chest had been gouged open, leaving a big red, meaty hole. It may have been the cause of death, but Harrison wondered if the metal fountain pens which protruded from both eyes and her throat, may have done the job first. Something that looked like a painting on canvas had also been shoved into her mouth.

He knew why her chest had been opened; it was obvious for anyone to see.

On the central kitchen island countertop, next to her lifeless body, was the killer's signature calling card, a broken ankh, alongside an old-fashioned set of brass weighing scales. The type with a metal bowl hanging on each side from chains connected to a metal bar. They were simple to use: a weight would be put on one side and the item you were weighing on the other. Once the scales were even and balanced, then you knew what weight the item was by how much you'd put in the other side. Only this pair of scales hadn't any chance of balancing.

Instead of brass-measured weights on one side, there was a single large, white feather. And on the other side, weighing far more, was the bloodied heart which had been wrenched from Kelly's chest – only it wasn't just red. It was red and white because it was covered in fat, wriggling white maggots.

TWENTY-SEVEN

Harrison had barely seen DS Fallon to talk to her, since they'd left Kelly's flat. They'd driven back to the station in virtual silence, the horror and implications of what they'd just seen percolating through their minds and turning the air sour.

Harrison had stolen a few glances at the DS as she'd been driving, wondering how much impact this visceral encounter with violent death would have on her as she still battled with healing the loss of her fiancé. The emotional pain of talking to Mrs Oaks had shown – not obviously, but enough for Harrison's trained eye to see. He was concerned about the pressure she was under after such a big event in her personal life. He didn't doubt her competence; he was more concerned about her mental resilience.

'We're going to need a briefing as soon as we get back,' she'd broken the silence in the car, her tone neutral.

Harrison knew that meant yet another charged encounter with Detective Superintendent Smith. But that was fine. It was a good opportunity.

. . .

The atmosphere in the briefing room was muted. Another victim meant the team were failing – and they knew it. Smith knew it too and made no secret of that fact.

'What is going on? We now have three bodies in as many days and you're no closer to finding the killer. Get your fingers out of your arses, or you'll find yourselves on filing duties for the rest of your careers. Now what's happening?'

Very few of them had looked him in the eyes as he'd barked at them, very few except for DS Fallon whose face was set and her gaze unfaltering.

'Sir, we are making progress. We've ascertained that Morgan Grainger did not die thirty years ago as had been publicly thought, but he has been ruled out of our inquiry due to the fact he's been living in Australia and hasn't been back in the country for five years. We are hoping to interview Paul Iverson, who was the person who originally gave the Set Temple information to Jordan and who we believe to be currently inside. He's got a conviction record the length of my arm.'

'How is that helping us? What's the motive?'

'We're still working on that one, sir. I'd just like to ask Dr Lane to share his interpretation of the latest crime scene for everyone.'

Harrison stepped forward and DS Fallon clicked through some photographs to show the image of Kelly Watts, or what was left of her, on her kitchen floor.

'You all know the importance that the Egyptians placed on their dead bodies, it's why they took so much care of them, mummifying them, preserving them, so that they could enable them to proceed to the afterlife. But they believed that one of the most important parts of the body is the heart. They thought that without a heart the deceased became soulless, trapped in the underworld and unable to go to their version of heaven. The heart would have been taken out and specially preserved then kept with the rest of the body in the pyramid, but usually in a special jar.'

The room listened to Harrison as he stood in front of the photograph of Kelly and the bloody hole where once her heart had resided.

'But to be worthy of going to heaven you had to first be judged worthy by Ma'at, the goddess of justice, law, order and harmony. If you hadn't lived your life by those principles, then you were condemned. To judge, Ma'at placed the deceased's heart on one side of her weighing scales and an ostrich feather, the feather of Ma'at, was placed on the other side. This is exactly what we are looking at in this scene that the killer's left for us.'

DS Fallon clicked onto the image on top of the counter with the weighing scales.

'As you can see and quite logically in real life, the victim's heart weighs a lot more and so she would have been condemned. To hammer this fact home, the killer has added maggots to the heart to show that it is not being preserved but is being eaten. In Egyptian mythology, Ammit, a demon, would devour the souls of those judged not to be worthy. The killer is making sure that Kelly is unable to travel to enter heaven.'

'So you think the killer believes in all this?' Detective Superintendent Julian Smith asked him, speaking up in the silence that had fallen on the room.

'Not necessarily. It could be an insult to Kelly and her beliefs and a message that they believe her to be a liar and unjust.'

'What about the pens, why the pens?' DS Fallon asked him now, showing a closer image of Kelly's head.

'Ah yes, that is yet another link to the group. They had all taken the names of Egyptian deities, which is common in the Temple of Set. Ellie was Nehebkau, snake god. She was killed by cobras. Jordan was Ba-Pef, god of terror, and his method of death must have meant he'd been waiting and knowing that he was going to die. He'd have watched the killer set up the spike, must have tried to tell the others when they came in not to come towards him. He'd have probably spent hours absolutely terri-fied waiting to die. But the others were also scared by the growling and the mist. And, finally, Kelly.' Harrison nodded to the image. 'She took on the name of Seshat, goddess of writing, wisdom and knowledge. Hence the three fountain pens in her eyes and throat, which may well have been what killed her before her attacker removed her heart.'

'Sick, the whole thing,' one of the officers exclaimed, shaking his head.

'How does any of this help us find out who the killer is?' Detective Superintendent Julian Smith frowned. 'Ron Norman was right. They were a bunch of satanic students, we should have brought them to justice thirty years ago and then none of this would be happening.'

'With all due respect, sir—' DS Fallon tried, but he talked over her.

'Perhaps we need to get Bruce on this too, help you out,' he said pointedly to Melinda. He was referring to her colleague DS Bruce Hewitt. She said nothing further, the tension in her jaw showing her thoughts instead.

'We have to look at the group itself,' Harrison broke the tension. 'Whoever is doing this knows a lot about what happened thirty years ago. All of them have said they've not talked about it to people; it's something they've tried to forget. Their alternative names weren't in the media, I've checked that. I haven't even seen them mentioned in the sparse records we have here from the aborted inquiry. We know it's not Morgan Grainger or his family. It has to be someone who knew them very well thirty years ago, or one of them.'

'Well if we don't get a move on, it's going to be pretty obvi-ous, isn't it? There's not going to be any of them left except maybe one – the killer! We've already lost three of them,' the Detective Superintendent bit back. 'How did the killer gain entry to Ms Watt's flat, do we know that?'

'Yes, sir,' DS Fallon replied, bringing up another image on the screen. 'They pretended to be a forensic officer, covered from head to toe with just their eyes showing. Means we can't identify them and we're also likely to struggle to get any DNA from the scene. With reference to your comment before, I'd like permission to have all four remaining members of the group put under surveillance. We are checking all their alibis for the murders of Ellie and Kelly, but the only way we can protect any more potential victims and catch the killer is to keep a watch on them.'

'And what budget is that going to be coming from? Do we even have the manpower?'

'I've worked out a schedule, sir.' DS Fallon clearly tried to keep calm in the face of all his negativity.

'Come and talk to me after,' he replied dismissively. 'I think you lot need to get back to the drawing board and find this killer now.'

Smith started to stomp out of the room like an iceberg cutting a ravine through rock. Harrison followed after him. He needed a word and didn't want anyone else listening in.

TWENTY-EIGHT

The pathologist dropped all her other work and had Kelly Watts on her examination table as soon as forensics released the body from the scene. The heart went too and as soon as she'd got some preliminary results, she called DS Fallon and invited her and Harrison back to her lab.

'Well, I can tell you that whoever did this doesn't have any medical knowledge,' Betty said to them both. 'They butchered her to try and get the heart out. Right mess.'

'Any idea if she was dead before they started that?' Melinda Fallon was a couple of feet away from the metal gurney and winced as she said it, looking at the mess that was once Kelly Watts.

'It's difficult for me to tell due to the butchery – I might need some more time, but I am finding blood in her lungs which indicates to me that the pen in her throat was before she died. If you were to push me on it, then I'd say that the pens were what killed her, maybe not immediately. She'd have had a hole in her windpipe and been breathing in blood. She'd have slowly choked and suffocated. What isn't clear yet is if the pens in her

eyes caused brain damage that may have rendered her unconscious or brain dead before anyway.'

'And the critical time of death? We need it to work out
alibis.'

'You know that we can't pinpoint it; my best estimate based
on the temperature in her flat, and the state of the remains, is
sometime yesterday afternoon. If I was to stick my neck out,
early to mid-afternoon. However, if we can get this heart over to
a specialist, they might be able to work out a more accurate time
thanks to our maggot friends here. They were obviously
deposited on the heart, and they've been busy already.'

Beside him, Harrison saw Melinda put her hand to her
mouth and make a small choking sound as she nearly retched.

'Have you got whatever it was in her mouth out yet?'
Harrison asked, keen to know and to change the subject.

'Yes, it's over here. Some kind of Egyptian mythological
creature maybe?'

Harrison followed her over to a metal dish in which a
canvas image was lying. He recognised it straight away.

'It's Ammit, devourer of the dead. Head of a crocodile, fore-
quarters of a lion, and the hindquarters of a hippopotamus.
Anyone not judged worthy would have had their soul eaten by
him. Another part of the message that the killer was trying to
convey.' He said this to the DS, who had gratefully removed
herself from anywhere near Kelly and come to look at the
picture.

'Is there anything else that can give us an insight into the
killer?' she asked Betty.

'I'm sorry, nothing else. Obviously, you can try to trace the
pens; I'll send that information over to the team, see if they're by
any chance rare and easy to trace. Other than that, not a lot. No
defensive wounds, so I'd say she was taken by surprise. A
couple of grazes on her head and arms, most probably because
she'd have fallen during the attack. I'm thoroughly checking the

fingernails but it's not looking like she gouged a piece of her killer sadly.'

DS Fallon exited the morgue as fast as she could reasonably do so, closely followed by Harrison.

'That was brutal,' she said to him when they got back in her car. She'd been silent all the way through the car park and it was only now that some colour was returning to her cheeks.

'Yes. There's passion and planning gone into her death.'

'Well they've had thirty years to work it all out,' she replied, not in a sarcastic way, but more resigned.

Her phone vibrated and she took it from her pocket to read a text.

'Right. This is interesting.' She became more energised. 'Paul Iverson was released from Wandsworth prison four weeks ago, but is listed as on recall because he's failed to meet with his probation officer.'

'He could be anywhere.' Harrison stared out the windscreen at the car park, his face blank.

'Yeah. Quite possibly out of his head in some drug doss house – he's got a long history of using. Or he could be who we're looking for. We need to speak to his offender manager, find out what state of mind he was in. Definitely someone to add to the suspects list along with the rest of the members of the group. You think he's a possible?' The DS looked to Harrison.

'Difficult to know because I still can't see what the motive would be and he's not got a history of intelligent crime. Doesn't mean to say that someone isn't using him as their proxy though. I've asked my assistant to do some digging on the group's backgrounds, try to put a more detailed picture together of what they have done the last thirty years.'

'We've done that. We know that Phil started work in a bank

and has been steadily climbing the corporate ladder, got married and had two kids. He's stayed around this area.'

'But you didn't know he had money troubles,' Harrison pointed out. 'Not until I told you.'

'No, true. But their lives all seem so anodyne. Paige had one job, met her husband there and got married. She too has had two kids. Dermot started working as a lawyer in London, clearly got disillusioned and has been an environmental campaigner, graffiti artist, and tour guide for the past ten years. Has an on-off girlfriend. And Andy, we know he went travelling, worked in cocktail bars in some pretty swanky places around the globe, then came back and set up one of his own. None of them have criminal records, the closest they've got to it is Dermot receiving a warning at a rally. They all seem settled in their own ways. None of them have flagged as being involved in anything like the group again, or shown any mental health problems. Andy told us he'd seen a therapist after the accident, but no other red flags on their medical records. I just don't get why and why now?'

'And yet there's something, something that's happened to one of them which has triggered this. We have to dig deeper. There is an insinuation with how the killer staged Kelly's death, that she was a liar perhaps. Maybe we can push some of the others to see if they know what the killer might be referring to. They're going to be scared by now, worried that they might be next.'

They talked very little for the rest of the journey back, Harrison's mind working through the information that each person in the group had given him. Rather than go into the busy incident room with Melinda, he excused himself and went back to his hotel room. He needed to work in quiet, to think things through logically.

TWENTY-NINE

The first thing that Harrison did as soon as he got to his hotel room, was to order some room service. He was hungry and his brain needed fuel.

By the time the food arrived, he'd ripped eight pages out of the hotel branded notebook and written the names of each member of the group at the top. Then he wrote down Paul Iverson's name on a sheet and put that on the other side.

While he ate his burger and chips, Harrison stared at the sheets, thinking through and occasionally jotting notes about everything he'd learned and observed for the various individuals.

Focus on the details. That's what he always told everybody, and yet they'd been running around trying to look at a thirty-year-old accident and three present day murders as one big picture. There was no doubt they were related, but it was critical that first he focused on solving Jordan Oak's murder. Ellie's and Kelly's would naturally follow.

Harrison's mind wandered to Melinda Fallon. She was doing the best she could, being really thorough, but getting test results and evidence took time, and it was time they didn't have on their side in this case. Then he thought about their conversation in the Indian restaurant and inevitably his thoughts turned back to the subject he'd been trying to avoid for weeks: Tanya. Ryan's news that she was thinking about moving away had ripped open the wound which he'd been trying to ignore and heal. His default was to avoid commitment, and yet... And yet the truth was he missed her so badly it hurt. He'd been faced with a choice: continue trying to find the person behind his mother's death and risk something happening to Tanya, no matter how hard he tried to protect her, or to focus on the living. On his life with her. He'd pushed her away, trying to get back to the status quo before she'd come into his life, but that door had closed. She was in there with him now and there was no getting her out.

This wasn't a dilemma for now. He had to focus back on the job and trying to prevent more deaths.

Food devoured, he called Ryan.

'Yo, boss,' Ryan answered, only it wasn't just Ryan: a small grey and white bundle was on his lap.

'How's Arwen settling in?' Harrison said, not sure who looked more content – the cat or Ryan.

He gave a big smile back. 'Just great. Follows me around the flat now, loves playing with her new toys too.' Ryan picked up a brightly coloured stick next to him which had feathers and a little bell on the end. He didn't shake it, careful not to wake the kitten. 'But I'm still working,' Ryan suddenly added.

'Good, anything else you can tell me about our group? I'm putting together some character profiles – you OK to go through them with me?'

'Course.'

'I'm going to concentrate on those left alive,' Harrison said, picking up one of the sheets and a pen.

'Phil Stevenson.'

Ryan looked on his laptop. 'Working class background.

Grew up on a council estate, an unremarkable childhood, but his dad lost his job when Phil was a young teenager, so money would have been tight.'

'He told us that his father expected a lot from him, possibly some of his own frustrations coming out to impact the son. Others said that Phil was hungry for money, with a background having no money that wouldn't be a big surprise, so it's a good motivation for wanting to join this group which promised they would rise above other mere mortals. And yet money isn't a primary motivation of the Temple of Set.'

'And now he's struggling financially himself,' Ryan added.

'I can understand some bitterness then, but a motive for killing three people? He was one of those who went first into the cave and also stepped onto the booby trap that killed Jordan. The other one, was Andy Lawson.'

'He's doing alright for himself, unlike Phil. Plenty of money thanks to that bar of his doing really well.'

'Yes, seems to have really hit on something and told us he was thinking of expanding, so why suddenly want to kill a bunch of people you knew thirty years ago and jeopardise everything? That doesn't make sense. He was injured in that cave fall though and said he'd had to undergo therapy.'

'He did a fair amount of travelling afterwards, went to some amazing places. I'll send you over a couple of photos I've dug up from about twenty years ago. You can see where he got the inspiration for his cocktail bars from.'

'He helped Ellie on their way out the cave. She'd tripped, and so the two of them were the last out. What about his childhood? As we know it has a huge impact on offender behaviour.'

'Again, pretty unremarkable. Did reasonably well at school, came from a lower middle-class family. Dad was a civil servant, mother a midwife.'

'He said his home life was fairly strict, but I presume no evidence of anything extreme?'

Ryan shook his head. 'Nothing reported by the school or authorities.'

'Might be worth me having a chat with his therapist and just seeing if he has any warning bells. Obviously won't be able to tell me much with client confidentiality, but he might say if there's been any dramatic changes in behaviour.'

'Dermot O'Connelly is the one who seems to have changed the most since they were at Leeds,' Ryan said.

'Yes, from law student to graffiti artist, although again I think that's a product of his upbringing. Said it was expected of him to go into law. We know that some people don't consider art to be a worthwhile career so that's not all that unusual.'

'He was a champion rock climber. Got into it at uni in his second and third years and went on to do competitions for about a decade or so after.'

'So likes the outdoors. He has a mistrust of authority too, some minor skirmishes with the law due to his propensity to go on demonstrations, and now a Buddhist according to him. Quite a long way from the Set days at Leeds, so does he think the others are evil for what they encouraged him to do back then? I also think that Morgan's reported death has weighed heavy on him over the years. That may have had an influence on his life choices. Might even give him a motive.'

Both Harrison and Ryan fell silent for a moment. Arwen lifted her head and yawned, before snuggling back down again on her human bed.

'Why now though?' Ryan broke the silence.

'That's the burning question. There's a lie though that they've all kept these past thirty years. The student liaison told us that Paige had blurted out that they'd not called for help immediately. Instead, they'd gone back to their flat to get rid of some evidence, before returning to the cave and calling the emergency services. If there had been some evidence of this, then perhaps they were worried it could come out and disrupt their lives now. Make them culpable for manslaughter, bearing in mind they all thought Morgan had died. Perhaps that's the lie that the killer is referring to with Kelly Watt's death, or maybe I'm reading too much into it.'

'What evidence do you think they got rid of?'

'No idea. May not have even been anything too awful as they'd have just panicked, but unless one of them tells us, we're not going to know. How does that give a motive for murder though?'

Neither of them answered.

'What about Paige?' Ryan asked.

'We have CCTV of both the delivery driver for the snakes, and the forensic officer who killed Kelly. Definitely not the build of Paige Nicholson, she's petite.'

'Maybe she gets someone else to do her dirty work.'

'Maybe.' Harrison sighed. 'It's here somewhere,' he said, staring at the detailed notes he'd made for each of the group members. 'There's something we're not seeing.'

He leant back in the chair and pulled his hands through his hair. At that moment, his phone rang.

'It's DS Fallon,' he said to Ryan, 'I'll talk to you later.'

Only, Harrison wished he'd not answered the call from the DS because it wasn't good news.

THIRTY

Paige Nicholson had been dragged from the bottom of their little ornamental lake by her husband, Tim, who had desperately attempted to resuscitate her before realising she was well beyond his help. He'd collapsed beside his wife with grief, but eventually managed to call the emergency services who had found him still sitting on the wet ground, sobbing and holding his dead wife.

DS Fallon thought Paige, now lying alone on the grass, looked like some kind of impressionist painting. Had it not been for the circumstances, she looked positively beautiful. Her pale skin and staring eyes looked up to the darkening sky. Her long hair flowed around her, wet like a landed mermaid.

Tim's visceral grief could still be heard from inside the house where officers were trying to contact friends and family and his doctor, in order to somehow appease the man whose life had been ripped in two. She tried to block out the sounds and focus on the job. She knew only too well that crimes like this had more than one victim. His life would never be the same again. It would always be half-empty and drenched in sorrow and regrets. His grief poked at old wounds in her heart and she didn't want to go back there.

Tim Nicholson was in no fit state to be interviewed, and DS Fallon doubted that he'd be able to tell them anything more than they could see for themselves. He'd told them he'd come home from work, gone looking for his wife in the house and not found her, but saw that the back door into the garden was open. Their ornamental pool was lit and so it hadn't been difficult to see her. He had a cast iron alibi as he'd been at work all day and driven a colleague home on the way back.

'Four murders. This is madness.' She sighed as Harrison Lane came up alongside her. 'We had a patrol car parked outside keeping an eye on the place. Why didn't they hear or see anything...? How did the killer get in?'

'The back garden is open – they could have come across the fields and come round the back way if they'd seen the officers outside.' Harrison was looking across the garden at the swarm of officers and forensic staff searching for any clues. He had thought about trying to track the killer. See where they'd come from and gone to, but even if he did manage to work out his footprints from the team's, what would it tell him? He had no doubt that whoever it was would have had a vehicle in which to escape parked up somewhere. The trail would lead there and then he'd lose him. There were times when tracking was king, when it could give him the edge on a killer, but today was not that day.

A doctor was kneeling beside Paige's body, signing the paperwork to legally declare her deceased. No matter how obviously dead somebody was, a medical professional was still required to certify death.

As he got up and left, Harrison and DS Fallon approached the drowned woman.

'So, no signs of any other injuries around her neck or on her body,' DS Fallon thought aloud. 'Looks like he held her under until she drowned. The lake isn't even that deep.'

'She'd have fought him, unless she was drugged, but she's only small – not much chance against a man. We might find something under her fingernails.'

'Yeah, and how long is all that going to take to be tested? The whole group is going to be dead before then. I'm going to have to take them into protective custody until we work out what's going on. I need to speak to the super.'

'We found this in the water,' a young officer walked up to the DS and showed her something in an evidence bag.

'Another one of those ankh things, Harrison. Only this one isn't broken.'

'Not broken?' Harrison strode over to take a good look. 'That is interesting.' He walked straight over towards Paige's body where he crouched down to get a closer look. 'There's something here, too, look,' he called the DS over.

Harrison pointed to her chest, where a small bulge could be seen above her left breast.

'Eric, Eric, can you come over here a sec,' she called out to the lead forensic officer who was talking to a colleague.

'We need to see what's causing that bulge.' Melinda pointed as soon as Eric had come over.

A frustrating couple of minutes passed while he retrieved some appropriate tools and got the photographer over to get shots of what they were doing and about to find.

A light was positioned for visibility and then he carefully pulled back Paige's top and revealed a metal, oval-shaped object. It looked like a fat beetle, wide bodied with two legs at the front and back and a smaller pair in the middle. It had been slipped slightly inside her bra for safekeeping.

'A scarab,' Harrison exclaimed.

'What's that there for?'

'It's been placed over her heart.'

'Why?' she asked him, but he didn't answer. Instead, Harrison stood up and paced to and fro.

'Harrison?' She was used to him not being the most talkative of men, but this was unusual behaviour even for him.

Suddenly he stopped pacing and looked at her.

'I know who it is,' he said. 'I just need to work out why. I'll be back. Need to make a phone call. You have to get the remaining members of the group in quickly or there will be more deaths.'

He didn't wait for her to ask any more questions, and he didn't give her any more of a clue as to who the killer might be. Instead she found herself watching his back fast receding into the darkness down the side of the house.

DS Fallon stood in the garden of Paige's house, the respectful murmur of her team around her. In front of her was a pale lifeless body, and her ears still picked up the sounds of anguish from the house. She knew only too well the cold grip that came with the knowledge you would never be able to speak to your loved one again. Never be able to call them to share something, to lie next to them in bed, to plan for a tomorrow. She'd been there only a few months ago and that memory was still painfully raw. For a few moments she was back in the hospital room holding the lifeless hand of her fiancé as the machines fell silent and he gave his last breath.

She was paralysed by the memory, wished that she'd quit this job months ago and applied to do something more mundane and probably better paid – certainly less stressful. She could have done anything other than this and made more of a success of it. Four bodies and counting. Just three more to go. She'd failed them. Failed to stop the killer. Failed to protect Paige Nicholson so that she and her husband could have enjoyed the rest of their days together for many years to come. Tim Nicholson's pain was hers. His grief was her guilt. Would she ever be able to bring the killer to justice?

THIRTY-ONE

DS Melinda Fallon didn't know what to make of Harrison's quick departure. What she did know was that she had to get in touch with the three remaining members of the group and ensure they were kept somewhere safe. But even that task proved difficult.

She arrived back at the incident room and was immediately greeted by one of her team – and it wasn't good news.

'Dermot O'Connelly hasn't been living at his flat for the past three days,' he said to her.

'No, he told us he was staying somewhere else, somewhere that the killer wouldn't know where to find him.'

'He's not told his girlfriend where that is either,' the officer continued, 'and he's not picking up his mobile phone.'

'What about Andy Lawson and Phil Stevenson?'

'We spoke to the manager at Andy Lawson's bar. Apparently, he took a call from someone called Phil earlier today – the manager was in the office at the time, and said she thought it sounded like he wanted to propose some kind of business deal, money was mentioned. Anyway, they agreed to meet up this evening but she doesn't know where or when. Lawson isn't at his bar and he's not answering either his home phone or his mobile.'

'Have you called Phil's wife?'

'Yes. No answer at their home phone, but we spoke to a neighbour and the wife and kids left yesterday to go and stay with her mother. She gave us a mobile number for her and she's confirmed that this is where they're staying, felt it would be safer with what was going on. Phil was supposed to join them tomorrow morning once he'd finished work. She's no idea where her husband might be and is now obviously frantic. He isn't answering his mobile either. It's like they've all gone AWOL.'

'So we can't find any of them? We were supposed to have surveillance on all three. How can they just disappear?'

'Well, Mr O'Connelly had refused surveillance, as you know, said he didn't trust anyone. Andy Lawson must have gone out of a different exit of his bar to the one we were expecting, and our tail lost Phil Stevenson when he drove into town.'

'What the hell; lost him?'

'Yes, the officer was very apologetic but they've not had any training in that kind of work.'

'I thought the boss was going to get extra specialist resources to help?'

'Unfortunately he hasn't managed that. We had to use uniform to assist.'

'What a bloody mess. We can't be sure if it was really Phil who called Andy. They were all duped once before by Jordan's invitation. Right now we can't believe anything is as it seems except that all three could soon end up dead unless we can find them now.'

DS Fallon swore and pulled her own phone from her pocket, quickly texting Harrison.

Can't find any of the remaining three. What's happening? Andy and Phil have arranged to meet somewhere. No sign of Dermot. We're trying to track them down.

'Where would they have gone?' she thought out loud. 'Get a team over to the cave just in case they've gone back there,' she said to the detective who was still standing waiting for instructions. 'It's unlikely but nothing in this case is going to surprise me so we need to cover all bases. Still no sign of Paul Iverson?'

'No. He's totally disappeared since skipping his meeting with probation. And there's something else you're not going to like.'

DS Fallon closed her eyes and prayed this day was going to end soon.

'What now?'

'One of the tabloids has got a new line on the case. Said that we have proof the group were practising satanic rituals thirty years ago and there's evidence of it again now...'

'Satanic rituals? What rituals?'

'That's not the worst of it, they're also claiming that the group didn't shut down thirty years ago, that some of them have been creating a network of followers, and that evidence has turned up in graffiti on the London Underground.'

'Who the hell has told them that? It's a complete lie!'

'They've got photos of the graffiti and say the tip-off has come from an insider in the investigation, but we've not linked it to our case, have we?'

'No. It's completely made up as usual, but it doesn't matter because Smith is going to go ballistic anyway because it just makes the story bigger.' Melinda closed her eyes and breathed in deeply. 'Right forget that for now. Our priority is these three men and making sure that no one else dies. We have to find them. Let's get ANPR, CCTV and every bit of intel we can, and try to figure out where they've gone.'

THIRTY-TWO

Harrison received DS Fallon's text as he was walking down the garden path of a man who had just given him the answer he'd been searching for. The motive for all the murders. Everything was falling into place.

His heart sank when he read the text. He'd been hoping that all three of the remaining group members would be safely in police custody by now but instead, more people could potentially lose their lives before the night was done.

Where would they have arranged to meet? It had to be somewhere that was important to them all. Somewhere symbolic. Somewhere where it all began.

Harrison called DS Fallon.

'What was the pub that they all met in the first night they agreed to form the group?'

'Harrison!' There was silence on the phone for a moment while DS Fallon's brain caught up with what he was asking. 'Pub?'

'Yes, several of them mentioned that it wasn't until they'd gone out for a night to a pub that they all sat down and agreed to form the group.'

'I remember. Hang on, I'll look in the interview transcripts, but first you need to tell me where you've been and who and why you think you know who the killer is.'

Twenty minutes later, Harrison pulled up outside The Hungry Hog pub, which was a ten-minute walk from the Leeds University halls of residence where the group had lived thirty years ago. The pub had undoubtedly undergone some modernisation since then, not least the fact that smoking had been banned and most pubs had needed to adapt by adding food as a service in order to stay in business. Today's university students weren't as heavy drinkers as they had been thirty years ago when Happy Hours had been more than enough to tempt them out and supermarkets hadn't offered cheap booze to consume in their rooms. Cheap recreational drugs hadn't been quite as widespread either.

The Hungry Hog was one of those older establishments which had no doubt been a spit and sawdust kind of pub in the old days, catering for the working-class men who would have spilled out the mills and small factories on a Friday night to drink a good portion of their week's wages before heading home to their wives and children. It had tried to make more of its heritage, adding some faux old-world props and black and white photographs of hardworking people long forgotten and buried. It also still clearly tried to appeal to modern-day students with a board outside announcing that they welcomed new students and had special discounts for food. As the new cohort had yet to arrive for freshers' week, when Harrison pushed the door open and went inside, he found the pub was quiet.

He quickly scanned the bar. He didn't see anyone he was hoping to find. Harrison walked through to the seated area where people could have a meal. Only one table was occupied – by a young couple clearly out on a date night.

As he turned back to the bar, the door opened and DS Fallon walked in. She spotted him immediately.

'They're not here,' he said to her.

'Have you asked the bar staff if they've been in?'

'Not yet.'

Melinda strode up to the bar counter where two young men were looking bored. One was idly wiping a glass and the other looking at his phone. They stood up straighter as she approached and pushed her phone towards them across the bar top.

'Have either of you seen these men in here tonight?' She swiped through several photographs on her phone. 'Detective Melinda Fallon,' she added pulling out her ID to qualify why she might be asking.

'Yeah. Two of them were sat over there. Left about ten or fifteen minutes ago.'

'Which two?'

'Him and him,' the more vocal of the two said, nodding when she swiped the photos again.

'Don't suppose you know where they went?'

Two heads shook.

'Has the university started back yet?' Harrison asked. He'd come up alongside her as she'd been talking.

'No, it's next week that they start arriving,' one of the bar men replied.

'They'll have gone back to the halls where they stayed,' Harrison said to DS Fallon as they walked back outside.

'How can you be so sure of that?'

'Because the killer wants closure and that means revisiting where everything happened – but this time being in control. Thirty years or so ago, they came here to this pub and then returned to their rooms a group that had decided to go on a journey together. They're going to want to relive that moment and put an end to it.'

'Right, well we need to wait until the firearms squad and tactical team have arrived on site,' she said to him. 'They could well be armed. I'll update them now.'

DS Fallon turned and spoke into her police radio, updating control on their next move. When she looked back up, Harrison had gone.

She looked around the street, stunned that he'd disappeared like a ghost without a word. What she didn't know was that Harrison Lane was never very good at following orders and doing things by the book, especially when a life was at risk.

THIRTY-THREE

Harrison had set off at a fast jog towards the halls of residence, which he could see a couple of streets away. Time was ticking on. Chances were, the killer was already taking another life as they stood there waiting for backup. He couldn't waste time: one or two peoples' lives could depend on him.

He passed a newer block, the streets and walkways well-lit for student safety, but it was like a rabbit warren to negotiate and he'd had to retrace his steps after going in the wrong direction. Then up ahead he spotted the large red brick buildings which he knew to be the accommodation known as Charles Morris Hall. Although updated since the group had been here, this was one of the older purpose-built student halls, constructed in the mid 1960s. As he'd jogged, Harrison had texted Ryan for the exact room that the group had lived in thirty years ago. He needn't have feared that kitten Arwen was distracting his assistant, because Ryan pinged back the information almost immediately.

The flat that had once accommodated them was on the second floor and Harrison could see lights on in the corridor. Without getting in there he had no way of knowing which windows belonged to the flat that had been theirs; but the biggest question was how did they get in?

Harrison tried the front door, not surprisingly it was locked. He pressed the buzzer but the reception desk was in darkness. The students weren't due back yet and so the place wasn't fully staffed. He stepped back from underneath the white porch area where he'd been standing and looked up.

On the first and second floor, windows were opened, probably airing the place out, but there was no way he'd fit through them even if he did climb up. He walked around the side of the building, scanning for a broken window, or any possible means of access. If the killer had been their usual prepared self and somehow stolen or got hold of a pass to get into the building, then that was going to make it extremely difficult for Harrison. He hoped that they'd perhaps broken in and he could follow inside by the same route but walking along the building, he saw no signs of forced entry.

As he turned the corner to the back, however, his prayers were answered. There were several builder/decorator vans parked up, obviously working late to fit in last-minute repairs before the start of the student calendar. Harrison walked up towards them, keeping to the shadows until he'd made up his mind what his next move would be. There was a low murmur of men's voices, and the smell of cigarettes. Just the other side of the vans he could see smoke rising up. Some of the workmen must have come out to have a cigarette break. He could go up and speak to them, show his badge and say he needed to get in, but that would waste time. They'd have to get permission probably and there might be some jobsworth who would refuse to let him in without a warrant. All it needed was someone who didn't like the police because they'd been on the wrong side of the law. Instead Harrison saw another opportunity. Clearly fed up with needing to punch in the code for the back door, or because they kept forgetting it, the smokers had left it very slightly ajar by propping a paint brush in-between the door jamb and the door. It was what he needed. He opened it quietly and slipped inside.

The sound of more men's voices – coming from the direction of the canteen, according to the signs – met him as soon as he walked into the main building. These weren't who he was looking for. He could tell by the accents and the topics of conversation, that this was the rest of the decorating team. He didn't want them to see him because that would waste precious time explaining why he was there. Instead, he quietly walked in the direction of the dark reception area and looked for the staircase which would take him up to the second floor. Once he'd found it, he ran up the stairs, taking them two steps at a time.

Harrison found himself on a landing with a long corridor leading off in two directions. Doors ran along the sides which he knew led to individual flats, each containing several rooms. Signs on the wall told him which numbered flats were down each corridor. Empty bulletin boards hung waiting for flyers about clubs and events ready to inform the next batch of students who would soon be arriving for their new lives – just as the eight young people had thirty years ago. The walls would have been painted since, facilities upgraded and the place cleaned, but it couldn't erase the memories and experiences of the students who'd lived here decade after decade. Today's events were a tragic consequence of that fact.

Harrison opened the door to the corridor on the right and before progressing any further, he stopped and listened.

There were voices. That was good, that meant more than one person was still alive.

Harrison moved towards the sound of the conversation which led predictably to flat 2B. The same flat that the group had lived in thirty years ago.

Very carefully, he tried the door handle. It was unlocked.

He texted DS Fallon.

In the block, voices in flat 2B. Door unlocked.
Will monitor situation but may have to go in if
anyone in danger. Decorators downstairs.
Some outside smoking back door open.

Harrison did as he said, pressing his ear to the door. He could have easily gone in but his own psychological training, and his experience, meant that he knew it could risk inflaming the situation, forcing the killer to act rashly. They might panic, thinking that the game was up, and kill immediately. Harrison also didn't know what kind of method had been chosen for this murder. The ingenuity of the killer so far meant that anything was possible and it could represent a danger to more than just the intended victim. The situation presented lots of unknowns that would be easier to manage if there was more than one person to apprehend him. Having said that, Harrison wasn't going to hesitate if he thought a life was in danger.

He heard one man saying, 'I don't know what you're talking about. We never did anything like that as a group. That's like the sort of thing they accused us of in the papers but you know that wasn't true. It was all bull.'

'I remember. I remember that you all believed it would bring you wealth and success but Set needed something for him to help you.'

'No! Get out of here. That's just not true. What we did then was just kids' stuff. I can't believe you seriously think that...'

'I know that! I see it every night when I close my eyes. And you all lied to the police. You left Morgan and I to die in there. You only came back when you thought we'd be dead and unable to tell our stories.'

'No. That's not true. We told you. We panicked and we thought we would all get into so much trouble that we cleared any evidence from the flat, but we came back and we called for help. I know it was wrong. We should have called straight away and maybe Morgan wouldn't have died but we've all had to live with that guilt. We were just kids; it was thirty years ago. In the past.'

'It's not in the past for me. I live it every day. I thought I'd dealt with it but I remember...'

The tone of voices suddenly changed.

'Stop. Oh shit, it's you! You're the one...'

There was the sound of a scuffle.

Harrison knew he couldn't waste another second, as the shouts in the flat grew louder, he took a big breath and burst in through the door, ready for whatever he might find.

He followed the sound of the fighting, straight into the kitchen area. For a second, he had to do a double take before he realised they were both on the floor. Andy Lawson was kneeling on Phil Stevenson, stuffing money into his mouth.

Phil's chest was heaving, breathing rasped. He was choking, suffocating. Fear and panic had turned his face a mottled white and red.

On top of him Andy's face was manic, his pupils dilated.

'You wanted money, here.'

'Stop,' Harrison shouted, his eyes scanning the room for weapons, both ones that might be used against him and something he might be able to call upon if needed.

Andy Lawson didn't stop. He didn't even seem to see or hear him.

Harrison stepped forward and grabbed both of Andy's upper arms, wrenching him off Phil, who rolled over and clawed at his mouth, gasping and coughing.

'Get off me,' Andy Lawson tried to twist away from Harrison, suddenly back in the room but oblivious to the difference in their size and body strength. 'I have to do this. They wanted to kill me. Sacrifice me.' His skin was pale and almost translucent. The man looked exhausted, washed out, and yet his mania gave him more strength than his size would have suggested.

'No. Mr Lawson, I've spoken to Doctor Wagner and to Mr

Fitzwilliam-Martin. I know that you've been for hypnotherapy. What you are remembering isn't real, it wasn't true. It is false memories.'

Harrison looked at Phil Stevenson, who had stopped moving and gone very red faced on the floor, suffocating with the plastic notes in his throat and mouth.

Harrison had to make a decision and he made the only one he could, he let go of Andy Lawson and went to save Phil's life.

Harrison pushed Andy as far away from them both as he could, so he ended up the other side of the kitchen. He didn't take his eyes off him, but grabbed at the notes in Phil's mouth, pulling them out to clear his airways.

'You're lying,' Andy sneered at him, recovering from the shove and the anger and madness burning brighter in his eyes. 'The police said it was satanic, even today they said it again in the paper. There's a satanic network and they sacrifice people as well as animals.'

'It's not true, Andy, that's just newspaper stories. There was no sacrifice thirty years ago. The geologists proved it was a natural rockfall. Nobody caused it. The fact the group left you and didn't call for help until later, that was wrong, but you need to know that Morgan didn't die either. He's alive. Living in Australia.'

'Liar.'

Harrison was trying to focus on helping Phil, his fingers reaching into the dying man's mouth. He needed to stall Andy so that he wouldn't need to defend them both again.

'I promise you I'm not lying. His parents didn't want any of you having any further influence on him and so they lied to you. They said he had died when he hadn't.'

Harrison pulled some more plastic notes out of the back of Phil Stevenson's mouth and as he did, the man gasped for air. He didn't think it had cleared them all, but he'd done enough to enable him to breathe.

As Phil groaned and moved on the floor, Harrison saw the flash of steel as Lawson pulled a knife from out of his trouser pocket.

'I can't take this anymore. I can't sleep... The nightmares. They have to die or I will never have any rest, and if you stop me—'

'Stop, Police!' A shout came from behind them as several armed police officers crowded into the kitchen area.

'Put the weapon down, hands above your head!' The lead officer shouted at them both.

Harrison stood up from where he'd been kneeling next to Phil and stepped back, raising his hands, aware that he hadn't met these officers before and apart from the knife in Lawson's hand, they had no way of knowing who the aggressor was. Phil was still on the floor groaning.

Lawson turned to the officer who had just shouted, holding the knife out in front of him threateningly.

A point of light appeared on his body.

'We have a taser. If you do not immediately put the knife down, we will deploy. I am warning you.'

Harrison didn't take his eyes from Andy's face. The man wasn't taking any of this in; he was in a manic phase, his own world. A world where there was only one outcome.

Andy didn't even look at the police officer; he was staring at Phil on the ground and suddenly lurched towards him.

Harrison steeled his muscles ready to intercept. Taser or no taser, he would put himself between Phil and Andy.

The police officer holding the taser gun shouted but Andy didn't stop.

Not until the barbs of the taser gun shot out and into his chest.

He fell to the floor writhing as the clicking electrical current, shocking him, sounded out.

The knife fell from his hand and an officer quickly kicked it to one side.

The kitchen went from static stand-off to all action.

Police officers rushed to Phil in order to assess his injuries.

The taser was deactivated and three officers took hold of Andy Lawson so he couldn't make another move, searching him for any further weapons.

After that, it was all over quickly.

Lawson was hand cuffed and read his rights. The fight had been knocked out of him, but he still protested.

An ambulance was called for Phil Stevenson, who had swallowed several plastic bank notes and was still coughing and retching violently.

Harrison was also handcuffed.

'I'm National Crime Agency,' he said to the officer.

'I'm going to make sure this situation is under control and then check your ID,' the officer in charge replied.

Harrison didn't argue. They were doing their jobs and he knew it was only going to be quick. As the effects of the taser wore off, Andy Lawson had started fighting the arrest and it was taking several officers to subdue him again.

'He needs psychological help,' Harrison said to them.

It was at this point that DS Fallon arrived.

He watched her assess the situation and give some orders to the tactical team. Priority number one was medical help for Phil Stevenson and that was all in hand. Number two was getting Andy Lawson into safe custody without him injuring himself.

'Mr Lawson, it's DS Fallon. You are under arrest for the murders of Jordan Oaks, Ellie Robertson, Kelly Watts and Paige Nicholson. You do not have to say anything. But it may harm your defence if you do not mention when questioned something which you later rely on in court...'

'They tried to kill me! You should be arresting them. Why don't you believe me?'

DS Fallon didn't respond, instead she continued reading Andy his rights. By the time she had finished, the paramedics had arrived and the fight drained from Andy Lawson.

'Mr Lawson, we are going to take you in now and we can talk more when you get to the station,' DS Fallon tried to placate him.

'Andy!' Harrison called to him and walked across the kitchen to where he was restrained. A tactical officer stood in his way.

'It's OK,' DS Fallon said to the officer, allowing Harrison to approach Andy Lawson.

'Andy, your mind has been tricking you. I'll get Pieter Wagner to come and talk to you. You trusted him, remember? He made you feel better. The Recovered Memory Therapy you did has created false memories in your mind and they've made you ill.'

Andy Lawson said nothing, but he looked at Harrison, the mania gone from his eyes and replaced by tears.

Harrison sighed and DS Fallon gave the nod for Andy to be taken away.

As the paramedics hoisted Phil Stevenson onto a stretcher and carried him out to the ambulance, Harrison moved against the kitchen counter to give them space. Phil was doing fine. He'd survive. But it had been a bittersweet victory. Four dead.

'We found this on the suspect,' one of the officers handed DS Fallon a pass card for the university in an evidence bag.

'Thanks. I recognise this woman; she works at Lawson's cocktail bar. He must have taken her pass so that he could get in here.'

DS Fallon showed Harrison and then finally turned her attention to him.

'So, they arrested you for breaking and entering then.' She gave a half smile at the sight of him standing with his hands in cuffs. 'That's for disobeying the SIO's order not to go in alone.' Her eyes joked with him but then turned grey.

'No doubt Smith will haul me over the coals for this too but at least we've prevented another death.'

'This,' said Harrison holding up his cuffed hands, 'was not on you. My actions were down to me. And besides, I had to. I heard a man in distress. I was duty bound to attempt to save him.'

'From all the way down at the front entrance door?' Melinda raised her eyebrows.

'Absolutely. There are windows open,' Harrison replied and gave a wry smile.

She shook her head.

'Plus, you're not going to need to worry about Smith anymore,' Harrison added.

DS Fallon looked at him quizzically.

'I'll explain all later, but only if first of all you wouldn't mind asking them to take these cuffs off?'

THIRTY-FOUR

It was late by the time they'd contained the situation at the student flats and Harrison went back to the station along with DS Fallon to give a statement about what he'd found when arriving at the scene. While he waited for the officer to take his statement, he'd forwarded on some of the emails he'd received from Ryan to Melinda Fallon's personal email address. He also sent her the photographs of Andy Lawson that Ryan had found at a cocktail bar in Asia, a snake wrapped around his neck, and another one in his hands. It would be evidence that Lawson had lied when he'd said he was scared of snakes and further proof that he was behind the killings. By the time Harrison got back to his hotel room, it was the early hours of the morning and he crashed into bed. The final thought he had as he slipped into sleep, was that of relief. Tomorrow he would return to London and he would find out if the woman he loved still loved him.

Morning found a groggy Harrison, tired from the previous long day, but the thought of wrapping up his work here giving him renewed energy – that and a decent breakfast.

DS Fallon had asked him to come back into the station to give a debrief to the whole team. While there was some euphoria that the killer was now under lock and key, it hadn't in his view been a success: three women had died unnecessarily after the first murder, and there was a trail of grieving relatives. He might have solved the case but it had come too late for Paige, Ellie, and Kelly. He felt deflated and angry with himself and hadn't slept well.

It wasn't just the case that had made him frustrated with himself, it was also the cold creeping fear that he was going to be too late to apologise to Tanya. He needed to get back to London ASAP.

The wrap-up briefing was at a respectable 9.30 a.m., and Harrison found the room filled with members of the team – most of whom he now recognised. The atmosphere had totally changed since the last time he'd been in this room with them. The pressure had been let out the air and when DS Fallon walked into the room, there was no mistaking her newfound air of confidence. That made Harrison smile inside.

Detective Superintendent Julian Smith was already at the station before Harrison had arrived, probably because the news crews had heard that the killer had been apprehended and wanted interviews. He marched into the briefing room like he usually did, as though he owned the place.

DS Fallon was just opening the meeting. 'Firstly, well done to everyone who helped last night and over the course of this investigation. I know that the arrest of Andy Lawson doesn't take away the fact that three women lost their lives at his hands, but we prevented two more deaths. Phil Stevenson has a family, two children who could have lost a father yesterday. That's down to you and of course to Dr Harrison Lane, who was able to piece together the ritualistic elements for us.'

'Yes, well done, Dr Lane,' Julian Smith said pointedly.

DS Fallon ignored yet another veiled insult from her boss.

'Dr Lane, would you please explain what ritualistic clues led to Lawson?'

Harrison moved to stand at the front of the room.

'Lawson's first mistake was the attempted snake attack in his flat. As soon as I'd learned what the group's Egyptian names were, that attack never made sense to me. Jordan Oaks took the name of Ba-Pef, which means god of terror, especially spiritual terror. How he died in that cave would have been terrifying not just for him but also the others. The whole cave set up with the mist and the growling, then the very violent death of Jordan. All of it, designed to frighten.

'Ellie Robertson had taken the name Nehebkau, snake god, who was said to have swallowed seven cobras. Ellie, as we know, died from cobra bites. Kelly Watts was Seshat, goddess of writing, wisdom and knowledge, and she died from pens being stabbed into her brain through her eyes, and also into her throat. All three of the deceased up to this point had a broken ankh, which is the symbol of eternal life, found with them. A clear message that the killer wanted them to go to the underworld and not be able to pass on to eternal life. This was particularly evident in Jordan and Kelly's deaths. Both of their hearts were destroyed. The Egyptians believed that you needed your heart to be able to pass on into heaven. There was also the added message with Kelly where her heart was weighed by Ma'at. We know that Jordan started the group but that Kelly quickly began to take over the lead and indeed probably carried on with the religion even after the accident. By showing that her heart had been weighed by Ma'at, the killer was suggesting she had lied and continued to do so.'

'We also know that the group had all lied thirty years ago,' Melinda Fallon interjected. 'They had not called for help immediately but had gone back to their student flat to clear away any evidence of the group, before returning to the cave. That could have resulted in both Andy Lawson and Morgan

Grainger dying. For thirty years they'd believed that Morgan did indeed die in that cave and for some of them it weighed on their consciences. They were also scared that this would come out and they'd find themselves in trouble. Reasons enough for them to have gone back to that cave after receiving the invitation. Please continue, Dr Lane.'

'The snake attack on Andy Lawson didn't make sense in terms of tying in with their names. Andy had been called Nectanebus, who was the last native king of Egypt and also a famous magician. When my assistant, Ryan, found out that Andy had not only travelled around the world as he'd told us working in cocktail bars, but that he also worked with a snake act, his lie unravelled. He told us that he hated snakes; that simply wasn't true. But his biggest mistake came with Paige.

'We had been told by several members of the group that Andy was in love with Paige thirty years ago. That affection was clearly still evident, because although he still killed her because of her part in what he believed to be his and Morgan's sacrifice, he couldn't bear for her soul to go to the underworld. He left her with a complete ankh and critically a scarab beetle protecting her heart. Paige, incidentally, had taken the name Tefnut, goddess of water which is why she was drowned.'

'This is all very well, but why did Lawson decide to attack his former friends, and why now?' Detective Superintendent Smith was getting impatient.

'Once I'd seen the Paige crime scene, I contacted Andy's therapist. Andy had told us himself that after the cave rockfall accident he'd been a mess. He'd travelled, trying to run away from his nightmares, but after returning to the UK he'd realised he needed help and had been seeing a therapist, Dr Pieter Wagner, for two decades. I know Doctor Wagner, he's very well respected. I went to see him and he confirmed that Mr Lawson had been seeing him but that he'd missed several of their recent appointments and so had contacted him to find out if he was

OK. Mr Lawson told him that he'd been introduced to a hypnotherapist and had decided to try out a different technique. As soon as I heard the name of that therapist, I was immediately concerned, as too was Doctor Wagner.

'Sebastian Fitzwilliam-Martin specialises in Recovered Memory Therapy, a technique that has been criticised and discredited in many circles. Studies have shown that it's possible for false memories to arise in certain individuals. Research and reports prove that memories can be manipulated and re-interpreted and that this can be particularly pronounced when suggestive techniques are used to stimulate memories by poorly qualified therapists. There have been countless big lawsuits against therapists and psychiatrists who have used these techniques and yet Mr Fitzwilliam-Martin has been continuing to practise, despite lots of complaints about his work.

'Andy Lawson had PTSD after the accident thirty years ago. He has been trapped in that cave under the rubble for most of his adult life. With Doctor Wagner he'd worked through most of the issues and symptoms that resulted from this trauma, but I believe that Fitzwilliam-Martin not only reawakened that terror, but he allowed false memories and untruths to be created in Mr Lawson's mind, bringing alive all the fears he's carried with him for decades.

'Andy believes that the group were trying to sacrifice him and that's why he became trapped under the rubble in that cave. It's the theory that was put forward by DI Ron Norman thirty years ago, which was picked up by the press. There was never any evidence that satanic rituals of that nature were taking place, instead the forensics clearly stated that it was a rockfall brought about by heavy rains. However, for Andy he came to believe that false memory in his head and for him, the only way to stop his fear and get some rest was to neutralise the threat. That meant killing all the other group members. He also metaphorically killed Set when he put that mask on Jordan, and it was symbolic that it was them who killed him as the group's leader. Stepping on that booby trap was collective responsibility.'

There was silence in the room as everyone took in what Harrison had just said.

'We also believe that Andy Lawson used dry ice to create the effect of mist in the cave,' DS Fallon took up the story now, 'he has a ready supply that he uses in his cocktail bar. It could have been put into the pools of water that occur naturally in the cave and would have completely disappeared without a trace by the time we'd arrived on the scene due to the nature of its makeup. No forensic tests could have picked up any traces as it's just CO_2, but staff at the bar have confirmed Mr Lawson has easy access to the supplies and we are tracking the inventory.' DS Fallon nodded to Harrison to continue.

'We think Andy left a device in the tunnel that played the sound of growling and footsteps. He could easily have also set off a device in the small chamber where Jordan was, to play a recording of him calling out for help. He may not even have had to force him to do this because as we know, it's now easy to clone a voice with AI. Because the rest of the group would have only been focusing on the horror in front of them, they wouldn't have noticed a small speaker or phone hidden in the chamber. Mr Lawson was one of the two who stepped forward onto the trigger plate, thus making sure that it was activated. He was also last in and last out every time. It meant he could plant the devices, then pick them up on the way out. He could easily have disposed of them outside somewhere and then gone back to retrieve them.'

'We have all of Mr Lawson's electronic devices and access to his computer – I'm confident we will find a trail for those electronic recordings.'

'So you're saying that we've got no proof of any of this so far, that it's all just theory based on ritualistic mythology. The most we have on Andy Lawson is the attempted murder of Phil Stevenson.'

'No,' Harrison had had enough of Smith's negativity and jumped in before DS Fallon had the opportunity to reply. 'I think you'll find that Detective Fallon and her team have the evidence sorted to prove that Andy Lawson killed Ellie Robertson and Kelly Watts. Through solid police work they have put together his movements on ANPR and CCTV, putting Andy Lawson in the neighbourhood for all the murders.'

'So what about the satanic network? DS Fallon have you made any headway with that? This could be nationwide but I haven't seen you even mention the bigger picture.' Smith looked smug, standing up straight and folding his arms across his chest and staring at her, challenging her.

'Oh that's pure fiction,' Harrison again replied for her. 'It was a story made up to catch the officer who had been leaking information to the media. I only told that story to one individual. I've let DS Fallon know all the details, and there's evidence for that too.'

Smith turned a shade of porcelain and looked just as fragile, his arms dropping and shoulders rounding.

'You told just one officer?' he queried, some hope still on his face.

'Yes, only one officer in the entire team. We followed the trail to the journalist. There's evidence which, as I say, I've passed on to DS Fallon to deal with.'

It was Harrison's turn to look at Detective Superintendent Julian Smith with a challenging stance.

When Harrison glanced at Melinda Fallon, she was trying hard to contain the absolute pleasure on her face. Just an hour ago, he'd told her what he'd said to Smith, and had shown her the telephone call and message which Smith had then left on the newspaper's tip-off line, along with CCTV of him buying the burner phone that he'd used to make the call. Ryan had gathered more than enough evidence to destroy Smith's career if it was ever released, and most likely see him kissing goodbye to his pension plan. Harrison disliked anyone who tried to stab a member of the team in the back, and he'd already witnessed more than one occasion where Smith undermined Melinda as she tried to do her job. What she did with the evidence now in her possession was up to her, but it certainly shut the Detective Superintendent up: he didn't say another word throughout the rest of the briefing.

An hour later, all boxes ticked, Harrison went to say goodbye to DS Fallon.

'We've just managed to track down Dermot O'Connelly. He'd gone rock climbing in Wales, attempting to stay off-grid as he put it. He's a very relieved man, although shocked when I told him that Morgan is still alive. I think that one might take a while to sink in.'

'I think it will. Morgan's supposed death had a big impact on Dermot's life; hopefully it will be a positive one now.'

'Thank you so much for all you did, your support has been invaluable, in more ways than one,' Melinda continued. 'Pieter Wagner has already been to see Andy Lawson. I think we're going to be looking at an insanity or diminished responsibility plea, but at least he's off the streets and the others can live without fear. Wagner totally agreed with your theory about the Recovered Memory Therapy. I suspect Sebastian Fitzwilliam-Martin is going to be finding himself under review and perhaps facing criminal charges. We've already put him under caution and will be bringing him in for questioning.'

'Good, but I bet that Andy isn't the only life he's damaged with his false therapy. That man needs to be stopped. Does he realise he has blood on his hands?'

'He is adamant that what he does is good for his patients. I'm not sure we're going to persuade him otherwise, but a jury may get the chance to look at the evidence and make the right decision on that one.'

'And what are you going to do?'

'Me? Not sure yet. Your trap for Smith has taken the pressure off me, I can't thank you enough for that. I knew what he was like but I'd never thought he would go that far.'

'Ryan said he's had several complaints made against him and has managed to dodge them all. It's about time he was stopped too.'

'Yes, it's not just me who will be relieved about that. I had thought about transferring to another region, but I don't want to take the pressure off him. If I go, he'll just carry on behaving like he does towards me to other women. So I might stay until he at least does the decent thing and resigns.'

Harrison looked at the woman in front of him. She was strong and determined, but there was still a fragility which she needed to address.

'Will you also talk to a grief counsellor?'

Melinda looked away from his gaze, her face instantly registering the pain those words had stirred.

'You have to stop torturing yourself. What happened was not your fault and I know that if he loved you as much as you love him, he would want you to be happy.'

She thumbed a tear from her left eye and turned back to look at him.

'Yes, I know. And you're absolutely right. We have access to help through work; I'm going to speak to occupational health and book myself an appointment.' Her voice started shaky but strengthened as she spoke. Harrison knew she would do as she'd said.

His job was done here.

THIRTY-FIVE

Harrison drove back to London with just one thing on his mind. Dr Tanya Jones. Part of him was tempted to go straight to the lab where she worked and see if she was there, get this over with, but he wanted to do it properly. First, he went back to his Docklands apartment.

When he walked in, he felt the empty suck of loneliness pull him in. That had never been there before he'd met Tanya, but now, no matter how hard he tried to vanquish it, it stayed leering at him from every empty sofa. Every morning he woke up and found himself lying next to its cold ghost, and the silence of it was deafening.

He'd been so fortunate to have been left the apartment by his grandfather. There wasn't much he had from his mother's family, but he went in search of something else that he'd been left. Something very precious.

Then, he called the lab where Tanya worked.

'Is Dr Jones working in the lab today, or is she out in the field?'

'In the lab, do you want me to put you through?'

'No, that's fine. I'll come in and see her.'

'Would you like me to tell her who it is and book an appointment?'

'No. Thank you, I'll sort it.'

He didn't text her to let her know he was coming because he had no idea what sort of reception he was going to get. This needed to be said face to face. Only then would he be able to be honest and would he know that she was too.

Harrison took a quick shower and phoned Ryan to let him know he was back.

'Anything else come in?' he asked, hoping that his assistant would say no.

'Nothing new yet, boss. I'll let you know as soon as it does.'

'Good and, Ryan, we'll get that house sorted for you and Arwen, OK?'

'Thanks, boss. I've started looking around but no idea where to start really.'

'We'll sort it, don't worry.'

Harrison closed the door to his apartment and went down to the garage where his Harley Davidson sat neglected and waiting for its owner. His bike had always meant freedom to him – as though he could escape anywhere or anything. But he'd come to realise that there was one thing you could never escape and that was yourself. Tanya had become a part of him. If she rejected him today, then it would only be his own fault and he'd have to learn to live with it. But if she didn't...

Dr Harrison Lane had faced killers with guns and knives, taken on crazed fanatics with his brain and his brawn, rescued victims from fire and water; but he'd never felt as nervous as he did now. His heart pounded, not just in his chest, but also his head. He thought he might even be shaking a little as he got off his bike and walked through the entrance of the lab where forensic specialist, Dr Tanya Jones, worked.

Part of him wanted to turn around and ride in the opposite direction, not face up to the potential pain that could be about to be inflicted on him. But he didn't. Melinda Fallon's bravery in the love for her fiancé burnt in his mind, and even the joy and contentment that Ryan had from the companionship of his new kitten hammered home to him just how much he missed Tanya. Loving someone was worth the potential pain of losing them. Even a year filled with love and contentment was worth more than a lifetime of cold, empty nothingness – and he hoped that he and Tanya would have a lot longer than just one year. It had taken him a long time to come to that realisation, but he'd got there.

The receptionist recognised him immediately and let him through to the labs where Tanya worked. He paused at the inner door, looking through the glass, searching for her brunette hair. She was like a magnet for him: he recognised the shape of her, her mannerisms, everything that was her. Harrison Lane took a big deep breath and got ready to face the biggest challenge he'd ever faced. He pushed open the lab door.

If she was a magnet to him, then Tanya must have a radar for Harrison because the second he walked through the door she looked up to see him.

'Harrison,' she said, studying his face, 'is everything alright?'

'Can we talk?' was all he could reply.

'Yes, OK, let's go into Esther's office, she's not in.'

Tanya gave him a strange look, which was probably because they'd barely spoken in weeks and then suddenly here he was, looking like a man about to face the executioner. Was it a good sign that she'd agreed to talk to him at all? Or was it a bad one that she'd taken them away into a separate office? He followed her with slightly shaky knees.

As soon as they'd gone inside and shut the door, she turned back round to him and asked him again, 'Is everything OK? Has something happened?' Worry was in the creases of her face and in her searching eyes. Despite what he'd put her through, she was still concerned. That had to be a good thing.

Harrison took a big breath because his throat had tightened and he was worried the words weren't going to come out. He'd been thinking about what he was going to say all the way home, and now it was time.

'I'm sorry, Tanya,' he began. 'I'm so sorry for not committing to you when I should have. I'm sorry for not having realised it sooner and I'm sorry that I haven't been in touch.'

He stopped, waiting to see what reaction those words were having.

'OK,' she said.

There was silence.

'So what are you saying?' she prompted, creasing her forehead and looking into his eyes.

Then it just all came out.

'I love you. I want to be with you for as long as we can be together. I don't ever want to be without you again and I don't want you to leave.'

Tanya's mouth opened as though she was going to say something but no words came out.

'If it's too late, if you don't want me back then I totally understand,' Harrison added in response, unable to keep the panic from his voice.

'No. I do...' Tanya's face crumpled and tears burst from her blue eyes, soaking long lashes.

Harrison decided that he'd come this far and with a positive response, he needed to go the whole way. He pulled his grandmother's ring from his pocket and dropped down onto one knee.

'Tanya Jones, will you marry me?'

She looked at him and the ring, still speechless. A small gasp escaping her open mouth.

'It's my grandmother's ring,' he said, not sure if she liked it or not from her reaction, 'if you want a different one then that's OK, you can choose. I'll buy you whatever you want.'

'No. No, it's lovely.'

Harrison's heart plunged.

'No you don't want to marry me?'

'No! I mean yes. Yes, yes of course I want to marry you.'

Tanya grabbed his hands and pulled him up from the floor. 'I love you, you know that. But I thought you couldn't do commitment? And you know that one day I'd like a family, are you saying...'

'Yes,' Harrison said firmly, taking her face in his hands. 'Yes, I want to commit to you and to one day us having a family. I'm not sure I'd be any good at it, but I will try my absolute best.'

'You'll be brilliant,' she said, tears still pouring down her face even though she was smiling and her eyes were alight with joy. 'You've been like a father to Ryan for years. You've had loads of practice.'

They laughed and Harrison slipped the ring onto her left hand. It fitted perfectly.

'It even fits,' he said to her, 'my grandparents must approve.'

Then he took her in his arms and kissed her, and kissed her again. Harrison felt enveloped in love and warmth, every ounce of fear and loneliness was replaced with a feeling that at last he'd found home.

'Do Ryan and Jack know?' she asked when they finally broke apart.

'No, wasn't sure if you were going to say yes,' he said smiling back at her.

'Well you'd better ring them and put them out of their misery. They've been so worried about you. One thing though, what did you mean about me leaving?'

'Ryan said you were leaving to go travelling.'

She smiled.

'He did, did he?'

'What? You mean it's not true?'

She looked at him again and raised her eyebrows.

'You think I could have moved away from you when there was even the slightest chance that you'd come back to me?'

Harrison's eyes burnt and the tears that filled them did little to quench the feeling. He shook his head in mock anger.

'I'll deal with him later then.'

But they both knew that they'd be forever grateful for the little white lie that Ryan had told him to goad him into action, because it had been told out of love and concern, and just a little bit of desperation and impatience.

A LETTER FROM THE AUTHOR

Dear reader,

A huge thank you as always for taking the time to read *Silent Souls*. Harrison wouldn't be here without you, the reader, wanting to spend time with him, Ryan and the others.

If you'd like to hear about my new releases from Storm Publishing then you can sign up here:

www.stormpublishing.co/gwyn-bennett

If you want to read a FREE prequel to the Harrison Lane series, as well as get other bonus content and see all my book releases, then sign up on my website: www.gwynbennett.com

Finally, if you enjoyed this book and could spare a few moments to leave a review that would be hugely appreciated. Even a short review can make all the difference in encouraging a reader to discover my books for the first time. Thank you so much!

This is the tenth book in the Harrison Lane series, and if you've been with him since book one, then you'll know Harrison has come a long way since the start of his Ritualistic Behavioural Crime unit. I wasn't sure if Harrison was going to walk away from Tanya or realise that he needed to start living his life, but I'm pleased that he has decided to put the past to rest and to focus on happiness – at least for now!

I've spent a lot of time with Harrison since I first started writing his story back in 2020. His adventures demand a lot of research, not least because the various myths and folklore, combined with psychological theories, are all real. From Toad Men to Norse mythology and, in this book, one of the world's most ancient religions, I've enjoyed discovering some of the unusual beliefs, as well as exploring the intricacies of our minds a bit more; and I hope you have too.

Thanks again for being part of this amazing journey with me and I hope you'll stay in touch – I have so many more stories and ideas to entertain you with!

Happy reading,

Gwyn Bennett

facebook.com/GwynGBwriter
x.com/GwynGB
instagram.com/gwyngb
amazon.com/author/gwynbennett
bookbub.com/authors/gwyn-bennett

ACKNOWLEDGEMENTS

A big thank you to the whole team at Storm who have helped bring not only this book, but the entire series to you. In particular, Naomi Knox who has very ably supported me through the editing stages of this book while my publisher, Kathryn Taussig, has been expanding her family. Thank you also to Natasha Hodgson and Shirley Khan for their editing and proofreading, and Tash Webber for the fabulous cover.